By the best

Romanc... ...

🐛 🐛 🐛 🐛

"Mature Men Don't Obsess About Women."

Believing himself to be suffering the aftereffects of career burnout, Austin reasoned that time and work would rectify his preoccupation with Monica Skye.

Hearing a whistle and the repeated slash of rawhide as it whipped and snapped the air, Austin felt chills on the back of his neck. Monica. Though he couldn't see her, he sensed her presence.

Shading his eyes, he peered into the distance, looking for her. Appearing in the midst of a brilliant ray of sunlight, he saw her riding a magnificent chestnut stallion with the grace of a practiced cowgirl.

She was the most extraordinary sight he'd ever seen. And he wanted her more than ever. But just taking her body wouldn't be enough. He had to have all of her.

And Austin couldn't think of a more enticing challenge....

Dee J's

Dear Reader,

This month, Silhouette Desire celebrates sensuality. All six steamy novels perfectly describe those unique pleasures that gratify our senses, like *seeing* the lean body of a cowboy at work, *smelling* his earthy scent, *tasting* his kiss…and *hearing* him say, "I love you."

Feast your eyes on June's MAN OF THE MONTH, the tall, dark and incredibly handsome single father of four in beloved author Barbara Boswell's *That Marriageable Man!* In bestselling author Lass Small's continuing series, THE KEEPERS OF TEXAS, a feisty lady does her best to tame a reckless cowboy and he winds up unleashing *her* wild side in *The Hard-To-Tame Texan.* And a dating service guarantees delivery of a husband-to-be in *Non-Refundable Groom* by ultrasexy writer Patty Salier.

Plus, Modean Moon unfolds the rags-to-riches story of an honorable lawman who fulfills a sudden socialite's deepest secret desire in *Overnight Heiress.* In Catherine Lanigan's *Montana Bride,* a bachelor hero introduces love and passion to a beautiful virgin. And a rugged cowboy saves a jilted lady in *The Cowboy Who Came in From the Cold* by Pamela Macaluso.

These six passionate stories are sure to leave you tingling… and anticipating next month's sensuous selections. Enjoy!

Regards,

Melissa Senate

Melissa Senate
Senior Editor
Silhouette Books

Please address questions and book requests to:
Silhouette Reader Service
U.S.: 3010 Walden Ave., P.O. Box 1325, Buffalo, NY 14269
Canadian: P.O. Box 609, Fort Erie, Ont. L2A 5X3

CATHERINE
LANIGAN
MONTANA BRIDE

SILHOUETTE *Desire*
Published by Silhouette Books
America's Publisher of Contemporary Romance

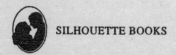

SILHOUETTE BOOKS

ISBN 0-373-76151-1

MONTANA BRIDE

Books by Catherine Lanigan

Silhouette Desire

The Texan #1126
Montana Bride #1151

CATHERINE LANIGAN

As a college freshman, Catherine Lanigan was told by her creative-writing professor that she had no talent and would never earn a living as a writer. With ten bestselling romance novels and praise from *Affaire de Coeur,* calling her "an unequalled and simply fabulous storyteller," Catherine has proven him wrong in a very big way.

Catherine is also the bestselling author of the novelizations of the smash movies *Romancing the Stone* and *Jewel of the Nile.* When not writing, she enjoys entertaining her friends with innovative gourmet meals.

One

Snap!

Crrrunch. Crrrack.

Standing naked beneath a slow trickle of icy mountain water in the outdoor shower her grandfather had built sixty-five years ago, Monica Skye did *not* expect to hear the sound of snapping branches across the clearing. Any unexpected noises could mean only one thing. Danger.

Adrenaline pumping through her body, Monica instinctively reached for her shotgun, and in one fluid, well-practiced motion, cocked and fired at the shadowy hulking beast across the clearing.

An almost-human-sounding wail pierced the air.

As the setting sun's vibrant crimson rays buried themselves in the mountains behind her, Monica squinted her eyes trying to make out the groaning figure writhing on the ground. She didn't need the sunlight when it came to sensing danger. She could smell it, feel it and taste it in the air around her. Living amidst wild animals for twenty years, Monica had learned to shoot quick and straight. With soapsuds slaking down her slender back and long legs, she reached around the trunk of a tall pine tree for a thin linen towel, one her grandmother, Adelaide, had owned when she'd lived in San Francisco before coming to this area back in the late 1920s. Monica covered herself to ward off the night chill. Modesty had no purpose in life-and-death situations.

Rushing into the cabin for the old lantern she often used when chasing foxes, wolves or mountain cats, which continually preyed upon her cattle, Monica investigated the groaning animal she'd wounded.

"Damn, woman! Were you trying to kill me?" a man accused in a pain-racked voice.

"Yes," she replied flatly, lifting the lantern high above her head.

Grabbing his thigh where she'd wounded him, she watched implacably as he glared up at her, still cussing and cursing like a crazy man. "Why? I didn't do anything!" He groaned and moaned even louder to emphasize the injustice of his situation as much as his pain, she assumed.

"Trespassing on my land was enough—"

He cut her off. "To warrant death?" He rolled over, trying to push himself off the ground. "What are you, crazy?"

Giving a terse half shrug, her wet, long blond hair gently slapped her glistening shoulder. "Some say I am."

Glaring at her as he rose, and grimacing with pain, he moved slowly still, mindful of the gun barrel leveled on his face. "Well, they're right! Ugh, God!" He clamped his hand over his bleeding thigh as if to stifle the pain. "I got lost, okay?"

"Looks to me like you're nothin' but a Peeping Tom," she replied menacingly. "You do this often?"

"Never," he said, gingerly picking pine needles away from his bloodstained new blue jeans and cashmere sweater, carefully avoiding further injury to himself. "Look, I'm not a criminal. I'm not trying to steal anything from you. I *have* seen naked women before. I wasn't peeping, for God's sake."

Something in the way he fastened his blue eyes on her shoulders and breasts told her he had been doing exactly that. "Liar!" She cocked the gun.

He groaned with a deep gutteral sound as he finally stood up straight. He was more than six feet tall, she guessed, and though wide-shouldered, slim-hipped and flat-bellied, his muscles were not as well developed as the mountain men and ranchers she knew in the area. Monica could tell this man hadn't done an honest day's work in his life. His handsome face was square-jawed and looked as if it had been chiseled from granite. It was topped with thick, wavy, chestnut-colored hair. His eyes were dark blue, almost as deep as the violet edges that outlined the Bitterroot mountains. Dark, winged eyebrows gave his face a determined, serious look. But it was the streak of anger that shot from his eyes like thunderbolts that kept her at a distance.

Monica had seen that predatory gleam in too many mountain lions and bobcats to trust a word this man said. "Just turn yourself around and get back the way you came," she ordered.

"I'd love to but I don't know which way that is. And need I remind you that I'm bleeding to death here!" he blasted. "I would appreciate it if you'd call an ambulance for me, if that wouldn't be too much to ask."

"What for?"

"I need a damn paramedic! What the hell do I have to do or say to get some human sympathy out of you?

She peered down the barrel of the shotgun, preparing to shoot. "You can have all the sympathy you want, after you leave."

Unsteady on his legs, feeling both pain and rage tearing through his body, he accidently stumbled to his right, crushing a clump of wildflowers that looked as if they had been carelessly strewn on the ground. Momentarily thinking it odd that this crazy woman would take the time to decorate her front lawn with plucked wildflowers, he asked, "Are you always this obsessively defensive? There's nothing on this broken-down farm I could possibly want."

"Ranch," she corrected, while not taking her sight off him.

"Fine. Ranch then. But it still needs a great deal of repair. I'd tear the thing down and start over, if I were you." He chuckled, looking around at the log cabin, the faded red barn, the pump and trough and windmill just beyond the barn. "I'll bet this place hasn't had an ounce of updating since—"

"Since 1928 when my grandfather built it. It's suited Granny and me all this time."

"Yeah? So, where's your grandmother? Maybe she's got more sense and will call the paramedics for me."

Monica motioned with the gun to the ground beneath his feet. "She's dead. You're standing on her grave."

Feeling creepy, he moved off the flowers back to his left. "Sorry. I didn't know."

"Seems you don't know much at all about these parts."

"Not yet. But I intend to learn very fast."

Monica was aware that night was moving in upon them. If she didn't get rid of this intruder quickly, she'd be stuck with him longer than she wanted.

"Since you'll probably never make it a mile with that leg of yours—"

"Which is *your* fault," he interrupted, blaming her.

"I'll have to drive you."

"Not a chance. I don't want to spend any more time with a crazy woman than I have to," he sneered. Pain clutched his leg in a vise. "I'll call a paramedic myself from my own house!"

When she shook her head, her wet hair felt like icicles against her back. "I know every ranch and farm in these mountains. I've never seen you before."

"That's because I just bought the Harrison farm."

Monica's mouth fell open. "That's impossible! I would have known about it. Their farm butts up to my property."

"That's precisely what I've been trying to tell you. I was exploring my place and stumbled onto yours. I had no idea we were so close."

"No one in town told me you were coming," she warned with blue eyes blazing.

"When was the last time you were in Silver Spur?" he asked as he glanced at the thin, moth-eaten towel that was now plastered to her lithe body, revealing every rounded curve, every mole and freckle. It was as if he was viewing her through a veil of a mist.

This girl hasn't got a dime to her name, Austin thought. If she did, she would have bought some descent linens rather than that old rag she's using.

"I get to town often enough," she countered.

"Good, then you know the way," he said brightening, and when he smiled for the first time, Monica couldn't help but think how his energy was enough to light the area.

She had to be careful that he was not one of those con artists her mother, Rose, and her granny had told her about. Men who wore flashy clothes, had fancy-talking ways and who punctuated everything they said with a smile were con artists, they'd told her—like her granddaddy, Foster Skye, and her father, Ted Martin. Men who "took advantage of a woman" and then abandoned her, leaving her with a broken heart. It was best to keep a distance and even better to keep a gun handy.

He was still smiling. "You can drive me to the hospital right away."

"There's no hospital in Silver Spur. Just Doc. But he doesn't take night calls. You'll have to wait till morning or take out the buckshot yourself."

"Buckshot? I thought it was a bullet," he grumbled to himself, but loud enough that she could hear. He glared at her. "I can't take it out—I'm a broker, not a doctor."

She thought his comment quite odd since she knew that *broker* was short for *stockbroker* and such people lived in New York City, not in the Bitterroot mountains. Her granddaddy had been a stockbroker in the 1920s though he lived most of his life in San Francisco. He'd made a fortune in the market and had bought this land as a getaway place. Monica looked at the stranger with discerning, critical eyes. This man was making no sense whatsoever. "I didn't say you were a doctor. I'm just trying to tell you there aren't any paramedics here, no hospitals and no doctor until morning."

"We'll just see about that," he said. Then he groaned again. "Fine. If all you're going to do is drive me home, I'll take that bit of charity. But could you hurry it up? I'm bleeding to death," he reminded her again.

Monica laughed. "You may be a bit wimpy looking, but you sure as hell aren't a bleeder." She started to back away from him, keeping the shotgun leveled on his heart. "I have to change clothes first. Don't you go and try to pull anything stupid."

Monica left the lantern outside not so much for the stranger, but for herself so she could keep an eye on him from her bedroom while she changed. She kept the bedroom curtains wide-open for the same reason. She didn't care if he watched her changing clothes or not. But she did care if he tried to move one more step toward the cabin. No man was ever going to step foot inside her precious home, filled with her grandmother's antique treasures and the sacred memories of her own life. This was Skye property, and under no circumstances was it to be invaded by a man.

Pulling a pair of old, faded blue jeans over her softly rounded hips, Monica zipped them up while sticking her feet in a pair of old cowgirl boots. After putting her arms through her favorite red-and-navy-plaid flannel shirt, which Granny

Adelaide claimed she'd bought in the thirties and which was soft as silk after so many washings in pure rainwater, Monica grabbed the keys to the truck her mother had bought second-hand.

Before leaving the cabin, Monica made certain the lights were off. Conserving both electricity and water were money-saving habits passed down to Monica from Adelaide and Rose. She knew every inch of the interior, as well as every tree and flower that grew on the property, and Monica could walk blindfolded across the large, but cozy living room to the door.

Just as she closed the door behind her, Monica heard a dog barking. The short blasts of impatience came from her Border collie, Daisy, who'd obviously just come in from the pasture to the east where her small flock of sheep had bedded down for the night. Daisy was a dedicated herd dog. To Monica's knowledge, Daisy had never before returned to the cabin before nightfall.

Tonight Daisy had found an intruder, and she was doing her dead-level best to herd him away from the cabin, away from her mistress.

"Daisy! It's all right, girl." Monica approached the black-and-white, long-haired dog with a smile. "He claims he's our neighbor."

Daisy stopped barking instantly but didn't take her eyes off the stranger.

"I am your neighbor. Trust me!" he scowled.

"Why should I trust you?" Monica asked as she took long strides toward her dark blue pickup. "You never even said your name."

Limping slowly behind Monica and the growling Daisy, he ground his teeth as he retorted, "You never asked me."

Monica stopped dead in her tracks. Whirling around to face him, her beautiful heart-shaped face scarlet with anger, she said, "You should have introduced yourself. Your upbringing is sorely lacking, mister. Perhaps if you'd done so, none of this would have happened.''

Slapping his hand on his forehead, his eyes were filled with incredulity. "Sinclair. Austin Sinclair."

"Get in, Austin Sinclair. I'll be glad to get you home so you can do your bellyachin' there."

"Do you ever give anybody an inch, Miss...'' he rumbled his question as he got into the truck.

"Not very often," she replied tersely. "And my name's Monica Skye. My mother wanted to name me Montana so's I'd always remember where I belonged, but my grandmother said Montana wasn't ladylike enough."

"She was right," he said grimacing with pain.

Monica slapped her thigh, signaling to Daisy to jump into the truck. As she started the ignition she cast Austin a derisive look. "So, you're one of those people who go traipsing around the country, runnin' people off their land. I've heard of that kind."

"I didn't 'run' anyone off their land. The Harrisons sold their land to me of their own free will."

"Humph! In all these years I've never heard them talk about doing such a fool thing."

Austin shut his eyes hoping to ward off the pain. "Look, since we're going to be neighbors, perhaps you could do a friendly thing...and be quiet."

"Suits me fine," she retorted.

"Me, too," he countered.

Monica looked up at the full moon lighting her way down the dirt road...looking like a shimmering silver pool suspended in a magical indigo terrain. Many times she'd felt a lunatic urge to explore the world beyond these mountains, but always she remembered that this was all she needed or wanted out of life, this was her home, and her roots ran very deep indeed.

She'd heard others talk about the hypnotic moon over the

exotic Mediterranean, or the beauty of an equatorial moon, but she didn't believe any of it. A Montana moon looked like one of those spinning mirrored balls like the one Granny used to hang in the dining room on New Year's Eve. They would wish each other health, wealth and happiness, Adelaide would tell Monica to depend only upon herself to make her own dreams come true. Monica didn't believe in fairy tales, moonstruck wishes or men who claimed to be trustworthy. Monica was a realist. Just like the orbiting moon up there, her word could be counted on like day moving into night.

Too bad she couldn't say that about most other people.

Two

Monica turned off the country road that connected her property to that of the Harrisons. "We won't be long, girl," she said absentmindedly to Daisy, who sat on the split leather seat of the rickety truck between her mistress and the stranger.

It made no sense to Monica that the Harrisons had left without saying goodbye. The loss struck a blow, leaving her nearly as sad as a death would. Any way she looked at it, Monica had been abandoned...again.

She'd miss old Harriet, the sweet Irish woman Adelaide had befriended. Harriet was forever bringing something she'd baked, canned, jellied or "put up" for Adelaide. In return, Adelaide had instructed Harriet how to quilt, sew, cross-stitch, knit, tat, embroider, weave and crewel.

Harriet had been Monica's link to her grandmother. With Harriet, Monica could reminisce, retell her favorite stories about her childhood in the mountains. With Harriet, Monica wouldn't have to ever remember those cruel moments at school that were imbedded deep beneath sliver-thin scars in her heart. Monica forced herself not to think about *those* times.

"You needn't pull all the way up to the house," Austin said, breaking Monica's reverie.

"I don't mind. Though I suppose it serves you right to have to walk that far on that bum leg."

Austin groaned loudly. "I do not have a 'bum leg.' I have an injury inflicted by you! Believe me, I'm just as anxious to be rid of you as you are to be rid of me!"

Slamming on the brakes, she shoved the gearshift into park and shot out of the truck.

Slowly Austin maneuvered his wounded leg out of the truck and stood aside for Daisy to jump out. The dog kept close to him, growling, ready to attack should Austin make a wrong move. He didn't know which was a more sickening feeling, staring down the barrel of Monica's shotgun or the thought of the dog's teeth sinking into his wounded leg.

He started limping toward the house. "Thank you for driving me home. Now that you're on my property, please leave. Or I'll get a goddamn gun and shoot *you*, huh? How'd you like that?"

Monica gestured toward the house. "You've desecrated the Harrison's house! What did you do? Blow the roof off, then set fire to the front of the house? God in heaven, it looks as if lightning struck the place!"

Austin kept limping past her without so much as a glance. "It's my place now. If I wanted to do that, I could. I paid for it, cash on the barrelhead." Just as he got to the opening where the front door used to be, Austin turned to face Monica.

"It's called renovating. I'm making the place better."

"Like hell you are!" she replied fiercely. Every bit of Harriet's and Chuck's personalities had been annihilated, Monica thought. She remembered the old kitchen with its white counters and black-and-white linoleum floor and the gas stove run by bottled gas and the house smelling of buttery baked goods.

Monica remembered the old German cuckoo clock that hung on the wall and Harriet's collection of roosters—porcelain, wood, plaster and china—that filled shelves, counters and windowsills. As a little girl Monica had gathered flowers for Adelaide and Rose, and she'd always included Harriet. Each time she made Harriet a chain of summer daisies to wear around her neck, the kindly woman had hugged Monica, kissed her cheek and sent her home with a spun sugar treat she knew wouldn't last the evening in the Skye log cabin.

Monica could feel the sting of grieving tears sear her eyes, but she refused to let a man, especially Mr. Austin Sinclair, see her weakness. Forcing her memories back to their hiding place, Monica promised herself she would discover the real reason the Harrisons left the mountains. Even if she had to go into Silver Spur and ask some of the "townies."

Of all the things in this world Monica hated to do, it was to ask for help. Worse still was being forced by circumstances to involve any of the townies in her personal life. To do so was tantamount to showing them her Achilles' heel, which sooner or later, one or all of them would attack. They had before, hadn't they? What was to stop them from repeating past history?

Had Austin Sinclair stayed where he'd come from, none of this would have happened. It was *his* fault the last people on this earth who cared about her were gone. She'd been right to shoot him. She felt like shooting him again.

Glaring at him, she repeated herself. "Like hell, Austin Sinclair!"

Shrugging his stiff shoulders with an arrogance he didn't feel, he said, "Kindly keep the rest of your opinions to yourself, Miss Skye, and get off my property. I wish to be alone."

Nerves still ajangle, Monica stomped away from the piles of building materials into the glaring headlights. Clapping her hands, she called Daisy to her side and held the door until the dog was inside. She slammed the door shut with enough force to make the hinges rattle. Grinding the gearshift into reverse, Monica stepped on the gas and pitched the truck down the rutted drive.

Austin had watched her walk into the bright, narrow beams of light like an alien boarding a spaceship. He'd heard tales about such happenings in this part of the country, but had always dismissed the stories as so much bunk. Now he wasn't so sure. There *had* to be some reason why this perfectly glorious looking human being was such a she-devil.

Still pondering the enigma of Monica Skye, Austin made his way through the gutted living room, down what used to be the hallway, to the back bedroom, which he'd converted into his sole living space in the house. On the far wall was his desk, complete with every electronic, state-of-the-art piece of equipment he could ever imagine needing. A single bed, outfitted in fine linens of navy and gold with a red-plaid-covered down comforter, sat against the left wall, and on the right was a brand-new, natural pine dresser with pewter drawer pulls that he'd found in Butte three weeks ago, when he'd signed the papers with the Harrisons for the title to the property.

Austin grabbed his portable phone and called the emergency number listed in the phone book. It rang fourteen times before it was picked up.

"Doc Kilroy here."

"Doctor, I was told you don't take emergencies until morning."

The man on the other end laughed. "Depends on the emergency and whether or not I've had my supper."

"I've been shot!"

"Judas priest! Where?"

"In my right thigh. It's bleeding like crazy."

"No, I meant where did you get shot?"

Austin's eyes rolled back in his head. "Oh.... Not far from

my home. I'll tell you about it later. Look, I'm in terrible pain, and I need medical help immediately. Could you send an ambulance right away?''

"Nope," the gruff voice replied.

"Why in the hell not?"

"Don't have one, that's why."

"My God! What do you do if someone is dying?"

Doctor Kilroy paused. "I don't know, son. I never had a patient of mine die in an emergency. Most times, they've been pretty sick for a while. Dyin's a natural thing in that case."

No question about it, I'm on another planet, Austin thought. He was more frustrated with this man than he had been with Monica. Maybe his decision to move here should have been based upon more rational thinking than simply the fact that the Harrison farmhouse looked out over the most scenic mountain view he'd ever seen in his life. Perhaps he should have investigated the neighbors more thoroughly. Then he wouldn't be standing here tying a tourniquet around his thigh and trying to reason with some buffoon on the phone who claimed to be an educated medical doctor.

Austin's mouth went dry, but he asked, "Can you help me tonight or not?"

"Certainly, son. But you'll have to drive here to me. My truck's got a broken axle. Sam Belton says it'll be fixed good as new in a couple of days."

"I can be there in a half hour," Austin replied.

"That'll be fine. Just so's I can have the paperwork ready before you get here, what's your name, son?"

"Sinclair. Austin Sinclair."

"Now don't you drive too fast, Austin Sinclair. I'm not going anywhere, and I finished my supper a half hour ago. I'll be able to get that bullet out in no time."

Austin didn't dare go into a detailed explanation at this point. He wanted pain medication, lots of it and fast.

"I'll be careful," he promised the doctor and hung up.

* * *

Coming home was just never going to be the same, Monica thought.

Pulling the truck to a stop in front of her log cabin, she experienced a heaviness in her heart. Her emotions had been riding a roller coaster this evening. She didn't know what to make of the entire matter, except to blame it on Austin Sinclair.

But the truth was, he was only responsible for a small part of her problems. She wanted to think of herself as a free, independent mountain spirit who owed nothing to anyone. But no matter how much she tried to live that ideal, people and situations constantly cropped up, pushing her dream further out of reach.

Austin Sinclair's appearance in her life was just such a situation. Not only was the man a perverted Peeping Tom, he was a desecrater of history and tradition. Monica wouldn't be surprised if the man went about violating Indian burial grounds and stealing bones and holy artifacts. She wouldn't put it past him to peddle his wares right on the streets of Silver Spur! Yes, he wasn't to be trusted.

Getting out of the truck and walking across the front clearing, she surmised that he'd probably come to this mountain to hide out from the people he'd swindled. There was no other plausible explanation for his sudden appearance. She remembered all too well her grandmother's stories about stockbrokers who smooth talked old people out of their retirement funds, invested their money in shady stocks or, even worse, just took their money and ran.

Her gut reaction to people had seldom been wrong, and from the instant she'd seen Austin Sinclair, she'd pegged him for a swindler. She couldn't have been more right about this one.

And she hadn't believed for a second his story about being lost. How stupid did he think she was? Now that she thought about it, being a Peeping Tom was nothing compared to what he was really after...her ranch.

Dad blast it! Why didn't I see it before? He swindled the Harrisons out of their land. That's why they didn't say anything before they left. They were too ashamed. Too devastated and probably had no legal recourse against Austin to save their good name.

"He's got another think comin', Daisy, if he thinks I'd ever fall for his tricks!" Monica said opening the cabin door.

Daisy panted and wagged her tail excitedly at the sound of her name. She followed her mistress into the cabin.

Monica stared solemnly at the empty rocking chair by the fireplace. "How long will it take before I get used to the fact that Granny's not here waiting for me?"

Daisy barked and then sauntered over to the chair and curled up on the rag rug next to it.

"Oh, girl..."

Monica crouched on the floor next to Daisy, petting her. Then she did the one thing she hadn't let anyone except Daisy see her do since she was a child, she cried.

"I don't understand what's wrong with me," she said tearfully. "Ever since Granny died, I feel as if I don't know myself at all. The least little thing sets me off in tears. Just today while I was out with the cattle, I saw this patch of yellow buttercups and pink primroses. I completely forgot about my work. I got off Starshine and picked handfuls of those flowers and brought them home, knowing Granny would be pleased. The only problem is, Granny's dead.

"For the life of me I can't figure out why it's so damn difficult for me to remember that—I was right there with Granny, holding her hand when she passed over."

Monica's tears were streaming now, and Daisy moved to her lap and began licking her cheeks. "I promised Doc I'd take good care of her, but I didn't do enough."

She remembered Adelaide instructing her to never have any regrets. She'd said death was part of life.

Monica had heard all her grandmother's words, but she hadn't anticipated how much she was going to miss her. Holding Daisy close to her, she realized this emptiness was loneliness. The revelation was shocking and unacceptable.

"I have to snap out of this. Skye women have always been tough." She put Daisy down and began building a fire. "I'll make us a thick stew for tonight, Daisy. Then after I clean the dishes, I'll finish the ironing. I need a nice shirt and jeans for tomorrow, because we'll be going into town on business."

Daisy jumped onto the rocking chair.

"If we keep busy, we'll be all right. There's nothing in this world that hard work can't cure," Monica said, forcing a smile.

Three

Austin Sinclair limped up the wooden steps of the white-painted Victorian house where Doc Kilroy practiced medicine. He knocked on the leaded-glass-and-wood door.

Golden squares of light fell from the first-floor windows onto the wide porch that encircled the house. Austin could smell the grape scent of mountain laurel, and the sweet smell of blooming roses as he walked the narrow rock path from the street up to the house.

"Who's there?" a gruff voice asked.

Austin recognized the voice as belonging to the man he'd spoken to earlier on the phone. "Doc? It's me, Austin Sinclair. I called you about my...wound."

"Ah, yes." The massive door flung open. The elderly gentleman was as wide as he was tall, and that was saying something since he stood eye-to-eye with Austin's six-foot, one-inch frame. "You the city boy?"

"Excuse me?"

"City. What city you from, boy? No, don't tell me. Let me guess. Los Angeles? No, not Los Angeles. You're too pale to be a Hollywood boy. We get a lot of them folks around here, though. San Francisco—" Doc looked down at Austin's brand-new jeans. "Not Frisco, either. They don't wear blue jeans in Frisco, least not since the hippies died out or tripped out." Doc burst into a round of laughter at his own joke.

The man talked a mile a minute, and little of what he was saying made any sense to Austin. All he knew was that his leg was killing him. "Chicago."

Doc whistled. "Tarnation! You're a long way from home."

"Doc, I need help. My leg."

"Oh, right. Come on in," he said, and graciously ushered Austin inside.

The house smelled of old wood, lemon wax and apple pie baking in the oven. The entry hall was warm and inviting. Oil landscape paintings graced the walls of what had once been the formal living and dining rooms and were now used as a reception area and examining room.

Surprisingly, there was little evidence of the fact that this was a doctor's office.

Austin experienced an overwhelming sense of gentle friendliness, as if he'd dropped his pain and cares outside the door before entering.

Gazing appreciatively at antique gaslight fixtures, costly mirrors, elaborately carved sideboards and deeply tufted brocade sofas and Victorian chairs, Austin felt he'd stepped into another world, another time.

"You a collector?" Doc asked.

"Uh, no. I don't know much about antiques, except the market's been picking up for quite some time."

Doc showed Austin into the examination room. He patted the white paper-covered examining table. "Drop 'em first."

"Sure," Austin replied and took off his jeans. Wearing

plaid boxer shorts, he slid onto the examining table, keeping his injured leg outstretched.

"Buckshot?" Doc asked, peering at the wound both over and through his bifocals.

"Uh, yes, sir."

Doc chuckled. Then he laughed from the pit of his huge belly. He had to hold his sides to keep them from hurting. "Hell, boy. You could've dug this stuff out with tweezers. You don't need me."

Austin gaped at the man. "What about infection? And, I well…I needed some painkillers."

Doc's round brown eyes leveled on Austin. "Painkillers?"

"Yes, sir. Demerol. Percodan. When I had knee surgery, they gave me Demerol."

"Knee surgery?" Doc continued staring at Austin.

"Yes, sir. Torn ligament. It was a skiing accident."

"Hmm." Doc turned around and left the room without another word.

Austin could hear the doctor's heavy, lumbering footfalls as he marched down the hall to the back of the house where Austin assumed he'd gone to the kitchen. He heard the clanking of glass, the slamming of a cabinet door. Doc returned promptly.

Holding up a bottle, Doc said, "This here's Wild Turkey. This here's Black Jack. These are painkillers." He poured two glasses halfway to the brim. "You take the Wild Turkey. I don't waste my good stuff on patients. Now, belt it down, son, and I'll go to work."

Austin couldn't hide his smirk of incredulity. "You're kidding."

Doc shrugged his shoulders. "Fine. We can do this your way." He started to take the glass from Austin. "I sure as hell don't need to waste good liquor."

"What about the Demerol?"

"Don't have any."

Austin swallowed hard and snatched the whiskey back. He downed the entire drink in a single gulp.

"That's better." Doc smiled and put the glasses on the metal rolling tray next to the examining table. Placing his hand on Austin's chest, he pushed him down flat. Doc stuck his hands into a pair of plastic gloves and took several instruments out of a sterilization unit. Bending over Austin's leg he began delicately washing the area, swabbing it with merthiolate and extracting buckshot pellets.

Austin was stunned at Doc's gentle touch. He barely felt the sensation of the pressure of the instruments as they dug into his flesh.

"Who shot you, son?"

"I'd rather not say."

"Don't worry. You may be new here, but I like you. I won't say anything to embarrass you."

"It was a...woman."

"A woman? Ha!" he bellowed. "Only woman in these parts crazy enough to shoot first and ask questions later is Adelaide Skye, and she's dead."

"Well, it must run in the family, then."

Doc straightened up, holding a pellet in his retractor. "Monica did this to you? What the hell were you doin'?"

Austin rolled his eyes. "I'd rather not say."

"Judging from your red face, I'd say you're probably in agreement with me that she's just about the prettiest woman in town. Probably in all of Montana, but then I don't get around much."

Nodding, Austin answered, "Well, I do get around, and I've never met anyone quite like her."

"Brought her into the world, I did. I know everything there is to know about Monica. She is unique."

"In more ways than one." Propping himself up on his elbows in order to watch Doc's reaction, he continued, "What

I'm trying to say, Doc, is that she didn't even look to see who I was. She just…shot me!''

"That's Monica, all right!" He laughed.

"What's the matter with her?"

"Not a dad blame thing, far as I know. 'Course people around here say she's crazy. They say she's touched in the head."

"Is she?"

"Not as far as I can tell. What do you think?"

Austin looked down at his bleeding leg. "Frankly, if I'd been a woman alone up there like she is, I suppose I'd be pretty jumpy, too. She said her grandmother died recently."

"That's true. Addie was a fine woman. In her day, now, *that* was a beautiful woman," he said wistfully. "Addie had been fighting emphysema for years. She was in her midnineties when she died, as best I can figure. She came here in 1928, the sixteen-year-old bride of Foster Skye. I can remember as a kid always thinking Addie was my ideal of what a woman should be. She was an angel. I swear I miss her as much as Monica must."

The way Doc talked about Adelaide Skye, Austin believed the old man had been in love with her. "I feel awful about walking on her grave."

"Don't."

"Huh?"

"When Addie was dying, she told Monica exactly where and how to bury her. She was bullheaded about some things and that was one of them. She insisted upon being in the middle of the front yard so she could 'still be a part of things,' she said. Addie liked having folks around."

"But I got the impression from Monica she wanted to be a hermit."

Doc nodded. "Rose was the bitter one. Rose was Monica's mother. Taught her to hate anything that walked on two legs. Rose had a burr up her butt all her life. She never forgave her father for abandoning her, and she never forgave Monica's father for blowing into her life, making her fall in love with him and then blowing out again.'' Doc pulled the last pellet out of Austin's leg, applied a dressing and wrapped the wound with gauze.

"None of that explains why Monica reacted so harshly when she saw my house.''

"What about your house?''

"She started yelling at me because I was renovating.''

Doc took off the plastic gloves and tossed them into the trash. He poured himself another Jack Daniels and offered one to Austin, who declined.

Austin continued. "She told me that I'd desecrated the house. But you should have seen the place, Doc. It wasn't preserved and cared for the way this house is. It was clear to me that no one had the kind of money necessary to take care of the place. Hell, the roof was caved in over the bedroom!''

About to take another sip of his bourbon, Doc's arm stopped in mid-motion. "Whose house did you buy, son?''

Austin looked at him. "I thought you knew. The Harrisons'.''

Doc came out of his chair, sloshing his drink on his belly. "What?''

Throwing his arms in the air, Austin asked, "Why does everyone look at me like that? What's so terrible about buying the Harrison house?''

"They didn't tell me.''

"That's what Monica said.''

"Confound it all!'' Doc stomped his foot. "What the hell was she thinking?''

"Monica?''

"No, Harriet,'' Doc thundered, looking at Austin as if he should know what was in his mind.

"Why is everyone upset about my buying this house?''

"I guess it's because the Harrisons have been in this territory longer than any of us. They just wouldn't sell out from under without a word to a soul. What did you do to get them to sell?''

Austin stepped gingerly into his blue jeans. ''I told them their view was the most beautiful I'd ever seen. I guess they realized I meant it. I got them a cashier's check out of my Chicago account the next day, and they had the deed and papers ready to sign.''

Snapping his fingers, he said, ''Ed Lovett—he's the only attorney in town. I'll bet he's known all along what's going on,'' Doc said to himself staring blankly into space.

''Sorry, Doc, but I have to ask. Did I do something wrong buying the land? Is there another lien against it or something?''

Shaking his head, Doc answered, ''I wouldn't think so. The Harrisons were always very frugal, and the land has always been free and clear, it being a homestead and all.''

''So what's the problem?''

Doc's eyes were filled with empathy. ''No problem, son. We're just not used to much change around here, is all.''

''I understand. It's tough to lose your friends.''

''Yes, it is. Now, you take care of that leg. I'd like to take a look at it again tomorrow. To make sure there's no infection.''

''Sure,'' Austin reached in his back pocket and pulled out his checkbook. ''How much do I owe you, Doc?''

Doc Kilroy looked at the checkbook as if it were an alien. ''Huh?'' He waved his hand. ''Nothin'.''

Austin wrote out a check for a hundred dollars. ''Here. I'll give you the rest when I'm certain gangrene hasn't set in.''

Doc took the check, read the amount and laughed. ''Hell, son. You don't have to bribe me.''

''Bribe?'' Austin was confused.

''For this kind of money, I'll tell you where you can find every mole and freckle on Monica's hide.''

"I...I wasn't interested in— I mean, that's not what I was doing."

"Oh, really?" Doc wiped the back of his hand over his mouth before he belted down the rest of his whiskey. "Then why is it that every time I mention her name you have to fight like the devil to keep yourself in check?"

Doc's uproarious laughter was too much for Austin to take.

"No way," Austin grumbled, put his checkbook away and started toward the door. Stopping dead in his tracks he turned around, went back to the metal tray, poured himself a jigger of whiskey and chugged it.

"I'll see you tomorrow, Doc."

"Sure thing, son," Doc nodded and chuckled softly.

Austin smiled, slapped Doc fondly on his broad back and left the house.

"Amazing, my leg doesn't hurt at all anymore."

Austin drove home as sober as a judge. He guessed enough time had elapsed since the shooting that his pain would naturally have dissipated. It wasn't Doc's whiskey that caused his light-headedness but the vision of Monica Skye standing naked in an outdoor shower. He felt positively bewildered by what was happening to him, and he couldn't have been more stunned if he'd been hit over the head with a two-by-four.

Though he would never admit it to Doc or anyone else in town, it was almost worth being shot to witness that much beauty. Oddly, it wasn't her lack of clothing that intrigued him so much as the fire in her eyes. Was there something besides anger, besides a sense of injustice at being watched and besides the fear she felt toward him? Had he seen something else in those blazing eyes?

He was almost sure there'd been a sexual spark in her gaze. He'd seen it so often before. Not that he was the most attractive man in the world, but when Monica looked at him, he felt as if a main switch had been thrown inside him. When she was driving him to his house, even his pain and anger couldn't quell his desire. He'd tried his best to keep his thoughts concealed from her by throwing her off the track with his accusations about her being crazy. The fact of the matter was that his fidgeting and moaning had just as much to do with his physical state of excitement as his injury. He was almost sure she hadn't caught on. Almost.

God! She would have had to be completely asexual not to feel the powerful magnetism between them; snapping and crackling like a live wire. Riding in the truck, he'd thought he could see it dangling between them; daring him to make a move. He bet her cute little dog sensed it, too. That was why Daisy adamantly separated them; she was herding him away from Monica as if he were a preying fox. Or wolf.

Wolf. Austin couldn't help laughing to himself, because for the first time in his life, that was exactly what he felt like being. He wanted Monica, and he wanted her to know it. He wanted to know what it would be like to kiss her, deeply and long. Kiss her in such a way that he'd turn her world around. He'd like to be the one who changed her odious mind-set about men, and from what Doc had told him, that would take some doing. It was going to take more than kisses to wipe out the Skye family history. But he couldn't help thinking that, given time, it was possible. Anything was possible. Something told him the time and effort would be worth it.

Part of his challenge was that Monica was better at concealing her thoughts than he: a feat difficult to accomplish without a lot of practice. When would she have practiced duplicity? And on whom? According to Doc, Monica spent her time with her grandmother and seldom interacted with the townspeople. She would have had nothing to fear from her grandmother, would she? Monica impressed him as the kind of person who would die if she weren't natural and spontaneous. Yet, she'd covered her desire for him with anger, rage and indignation. But it was there.

He could still feel it. It lingered around him like heady musk.

He gripped the steering wheel as a wave of sexual need swept over him. For the life of him, he couldn't ever remember feeling this vulnerable to passion. Not even his ex-fiancée, Callie, had caused this kind of physical reaction in him.

Callie had made the first move on Austin, which he'd thought quirky, when they'd met in a dimly lit Irish pub on Chicago's north side.

It was St. Patrick's day.

From then on they were together. Austin couldn't honestly remember pursuing Callie. She always had social plans that seemed to easily include Austin. As time passed she didn't call and ask his approval any longer, she accepted for them both. A year later they became engaged. Six months after that, she left him standing at the altar. Confused and embarrassed, Austin had excused the guests with his apologies. He left the church, drove to her apartment and discovered Callie packing to move to Boston. She'd been offered a job with a top legal firm. Finally, after talking it through, he discovered that she'd been afraid their relationship would never work, that she could never make him love her.

Austin had known she was right. His breakup with Callie had been the beginning of his search for himself. Two weeks later he'd gone with Steve and Brad to Montana on a fly-fishing trip. Austin hadn't thought much about the journey other than the fact that it would be good to be away from the pressure cooker his life had become.

The intense desire to make money not only for his clients but for himself, as well, had kept Austin's nerves strung out for seven years. At the age of twenty-nine, he was already rich. His colleagues called him a genius and said he had a knack for picking winners. But Austin knew the truth behind his success. He was lucky.

There was something to be said for luck, the meeting of

time, place and determination that few understood and so discounted. Austin wasn't the brightest man in his graduating class at University of Chicago. He didn't work any harder or longer than other commodity traders, but he did work smarter. And he listened to every detail pertaining not only to commodities, but to stocks in general, to which he was privy. He paid attention. He watched the markets. He listened to his instincts. He researched companies. He researched weather conditions, read the Farmers' Almanac and followed international politics to know whether foreign subsidies were still in effect and if trade embargoes would affect grain, sugar, wheat or coffee.

Austin's other piece of luck was that he was lonely. Even when he was going with Callie, Austin felt lonely. To fill the void of not having a wife or children, Austin thought about trading.

When other guys in the office were wondering what gifts to buy their wives and girlfriends for Valentine's Day, Christmas or birthdays, Austin was thinking about new high-tech computer companies popping up on the NASDAC. He remembered dashing out at the last minute to buy Callie whatever was left over on the department store shelves, claiming an expensive dinner at Chez Pierre was her "real" gift.

It was no wonder that by the end of his most frantic and lucrative summer at Sherron and Bronson, Austin felt he was going to explode. Whether fly-fishing was the necessary cure, he had yet to discover.

Though the two-week trip had begun with Austin cursing during all daylight hours over the fact that his cellular phone kept breaking up out in the wilderness where there were few if any transmitters, by the fourth day, Austin had made two major self-discoveries.

The first was that he felt less lonely in the wilds of Montana than he did in Chicago with four million people around. He didn't understand why he felt the way he did, only that he did.

His second revelation was that the natural beauty of the mountains and valleys moved something inexplicable in his soul. He was in awe of every tree, waterfall, animal and bird. He had the strangest feeling that for the first time he'd come home.

For days he said nothing to Brad or Steve about the profound changes going on in his head—and heart. Selfishly he wanted to keep his wondrous discoveries to himself. He didn't need their input. He knew what he felt.

When they returned to Chicago, Austin began discreet inquiries about ranches, home sites and the like for sale in Montana. He spent five days at Christmas driving a rented Mercury Mountaineer over the Bitteroot Mountains.

It had been luck that had led Austin to the Harrison homestead, not his flat tire. It had been luck that the Harrisons had helped him with the tire and then invited him in for pie and coffee. Austin had been dumbstruck by the beauty of this particular place, but it was the powerful stirring deep in his soul that made Austin turn to the Harrisons and ask, "By any chance would you be willing to sell this land?"

They'd looked at him as if he were the Second Coming.

They struck a bargain and agreed on a price. Austin explained it would take him three months to wrap up his business in Chicago. Mrs. Harrison explained that she wanted to stay in the mountains through the winter before they moved to Billings.

Back home after his trip to the doctor, Austin pulled his truck up to the stacks of lumber and bricks piled in his front yard. He turned off the ignition and headlights. Walking toward the house, he stopped to inhale the sweet mountain air. It was so crisp and clean he felt his entire body rejuvenate itself. He looked up at the sky.

"Nobody's got as many stars as I do," he said, smiling to himself.

Without thinking he turned his head toward Monica's land, which rose up behind his like a majestic, purple-cloaked shadow. There were no lights burning anywhere that he could see. No old truck coming down the road.

Is she sleeping? he wondered. Is she dreaming? Does she regret that she shot me? Or doesn't she care?

Looking to the peak of the hill, he could see the full moon cresting.

She cares. The thought came to him in a flash.

She cares about a lot of things.

The ferocity with which she protected her property from him told him she cared. To Monica her ranch was as much human as he was.

Living in Chicago, Austin had never thought much about where he lived, or even if he liked being there. Geography was not his concern, he'd assumed, until he'd come to Montana. He didn't think like that anymore.

Now he felt about his land much like he figured Monica did. This place was his home. Here he'd found peace of mind in the whispering winds; comfort in the mountains that embraced the valley. Though he was in the middle of nowhere, he felt nurtured by an invisible force that defied description.

In all fairness, there hadn't been anything particularly wrong with his life in the city. It was simply that it just wasn't *right*. If he'd never come to Montana, he might have gone on living there, being content. Maybe it was corny to believe that he'd gone back to nature to find himself, but it was true. Maybe it was just wishful thinking to wonder if Monica Skye wasn't part of the destiny he'd come here to fulfill, but as far as Austin was concerned, it was an intriguing question indeed.

Four

Monica drove her sputtering truck down the mountain road into Silver Spur, where she had a ten-o'clock meeting with Jake Simmons to discuss the sale of her cattle.

Parking in front of Jake's office, she pretended not to notice the two middle-aged ranchers standing outside the general store watching her. She got out and closed the creaking door.

"What do you suppose keeps that old clunker of hers going, Will? It shoulda fallen apart twenty years ago." Perry Clay, the skinny man in overalls said to his friend, Will Abramson.

"I heard tell Adelaide ran moonshine with it."

Perry rocked back on his heels. "Moonshine? That stuff will rot a body's brain."

"Yep," Will agreed staring coldly at Monica. "Makes folks crazy all right."

Both men howled. "Monica musta drank too much of that stuff herself, thinking she can keep that truck going...like she thinks she can handle that ranch all by herself."

Giving them no more than a sidelong glance, Monica refused to let their slurs undercut her confidence today. She needed this sale with Jake to insure her livelihood for the next year. With this money she could finish repairing the fence, put new shingles on the cabin roof, fix the plumbing in the kitchen and bathroom and buy a set of new tires. She'd buy a new truck if she had enough money. Problem was, there had never been enough money.

Looking a bit farther down the block, she saw Moss Fuller. If she hadn't known better she would have sworn she saw terror in his eyes. He whirled around into Ruby's Saloon so fast, he looked like a spinning target in a shooting gallery. Across the street at the pharmacy, Bill Highstatler quickly ducked away from the window where he'd been watching her. Though she'd always been treated strangely by the townspeople, their behavior today struck her as being more odd than usual.

She entered Jake's office and walked up to the pine desk where Trace Southern sat buffing her nails.

Monica glanced over her shoulder through the square picture window at Perry and Will who sauntered toward her truck. "I didn't know you were working here, Trace."

Trace flipped her thick strawberry blond braid over her shoulder and replied, "I've been here since Christmas, Monica. I 'spose if you'd ever come to town, you might know that."

Peering through the painted lettering on the window, Monica watched as Perry kicked the back tire, but the act must not have produced the same kind of thrill as verbal taunting, because he walked idly away looking nearly as bored as Will. "I come to town every chance I get, Trace," Monica retorted as she turned and faced her old classmate. "I've been so busy, there's just not been much time."

"Busy?" Trace's thin, pink-glossed lips exposed perfect

white teeth. "Well, I guess that's right, isn't it? Shootin' strangers is time-consuming, isn't it?"

"What?"

"Word's all over town that you tried to kill somebody last night. You sure he was a stranger and not a boyfriend you've been hiding?"

To Monica, Trace's smile had always appeared slightly sardonic, but she'd chalked it up to Trace's pretty, though very sharp, features. Today she realized there was nothing unintentional about her comments. "Boyfriend?"

"You have had one, haven't you?" Trace asked pointedly.

Pride made Monica want to explain, but her inner voice told her she'd be wasting her time. "Where'd you hear about it?"

Whisking her hand against invisible dirt on the sleeves of her white cotton blouse, Trace said, "Around. You know how it is," she quipped. However, Monica's glare was as hot as a poker, causing Trace to cringe. "Why don't you ask Doc?"

Trace's answer stung. Doc was about the only friend Monica had in Silver Spur. She couldn't believe he would betray her like this. She wanted to confront him immediately, but she wouldn't give Trace the satisfaction of hitting her mark.

Monica had learned long ago how to steel herself against unwarranted attacks. She'd developed the hide of a rhinoceros, which she liked to believe was now impervious to barbs. She'd also learned that sometimes the best defense was an offense and the more subtle the offense, the more effective the attack.

"Hmm. Doc. Yes, I guess he hasn't seen a real gunshot wound in a long time."

"Gunshot? I thought it was buckshot."

It was Monica's turn to smile. "If it was buckshot, then I didn't really intend to kill anyone, did I?"

"Well, I...er..."

Trace can't parry with a goat, Monica thought and for the first time, she realized the former Silver Spur Prom Queen who'd twisted both high school faculty and students around her finger, wasn't a threat at all. In fact she seemed quite silly.

"I have an appointment with Jake," Monica said, changing the subject.

"He's not here," Trace replied curtly, pulling out a schedule book. "There's no mention of you here in his book."

"He knows damn well I come here every year on the first of May to sell my cattle. Hell, my cattle pay your salary, Trace. He better have time to see me today."

"It's customary to call and make an appointment, Monica."

"I don't have a phone," Monica said, her blue eyes turning an intimidating steel gray.

The acidity in Trace's voice vanished. "He has a haircut appointment this morning. Then nothing till noon. Maybe he could see you, after all."

"You bet he will," Monica said, taking long gliding steps out of the office and not looking back.

Knowing that Jake's haircut would take some time, Monica decided to confront Doc. It was best she direct her anger at the person responsible and not blow her cattle deal.

Sitting upright on the examining table, Austin crossed his arms nonchalantly over his chest while Doc Kilroy swabbed his wounds with a new application of antibacterial ointment.

"You sure this is good stuff, Doc?" Austin asked.

"Hell, yes. I used it on Sadie Dandridge's mare last fall. Healed up right nice." Doc smiled a Cheshire cat grin.

"You," Austin poked the old man playfully in the chest, "are a rascal."

Monica stood in the doorway to the examination room arms akimbo and with a searing glare in her eyes. "And a bastard to boot!"

"What?" Doc whirled around.

Austin cupped his hands over his crotch. "Monica!"

Marching up to Doc, her angry words spewed like lava.

"You said you were my friend, and I was fool enough to believe you all this time. It's just like Granny always said, 'Men will double-cross you every chance they get.' I believed her. I had no reason not to. Except about you. I trusted you, Doc. But now I find out you were just lying in wait like the weasel you are."

"Hold on there, Monica. What's got you so upset?" Doc asked.

Nodding toward Austin, she replied, "I wasn't in town two minutes and Trace asks me about the man I tried to kill last night."

"Kill?"

"That's what she said. No wonder Moss looked at me like I was a banshee. He probably thought I'd pick him off with a six-shooter."

"Baretta or Magnum, but not a six-shooter," Austin corrected.

"Pardon me?" She glared at him.

He smiled warmly. "Or a Glock."

"What is he talking about, Doc?"

Extending his hand amicably toward Monica, Doc answered, "Those are modern guns, Monica."

"I never heard of them."

Austin nodded. "Precisely my point. How could you be trying to kill someone without proper equipment?"

Monica looked at him quizzically. "I don't recall asking for your opinion."

"This just so happens to be my appointment time you're using," Austin announced, wishing she would go away at least until he could get dressed. "Are you going to pay my bill?"

"Absolutely not." Giving his leg a sidelong glance she saw the mangled flesh and winced. When she realized how he was positioned she was embarrassed for him, but she wasn't about to let him know it. Maybe he didn't have a problem with his near nakedness, but she did.

Ignoring him she continued, "What I want to know, Doc, is why you betrayed me? Why did you tell everybody I was trying to kill someone? Why talk to anyone about it at all?"

"I didn't."

"Don't lie to me, Doc."

There was empathy in Doc's voice when he spoke again. "I would never lie to you or hurt you, Monica. You're one of the dearest people I know." He put his hand on her shoulder affectionately.

Monica felt her anger ease out of her like a balloon deflating. "There's no way anyone would have found out about last night if you didn't tell them."

"Sure there is."

"What?" Austin and Monica asked in unison.

"I have to file a report at the sheriff's office for every gunshot and knife wound I treat. By law that includes buckshot. I filed my report this morning. If the sheriff decides to investigate, that's up to him."

"Investigate?" Monica said indignantly, and then she pointed toward Austin. "He was trespassing."

Austin didn't know when his mouth had worked itself into a smile, but as he watched Monica defend her integrity and her actions, he couldn't help admiring her. At that moment when she turned on him, her eyes flashing like blue crystals, she halted momentarily, sucking in her breath when she read his thoughts. And Austin was transfixed.

Austin had not only surprised Monica, he'd impressed her. She stumbled over her words, telling him she was having a hard time picking up her train of thought. She hadn't expected him to be her champion, but that was how it felt to her.

She'd wanted to shove him in that convenient box of adversaries where she kept everyone but Granny. She was comfortable with her world of black and white, right and wrong, herself against the world. But Austin Sinclair looked at her as if she'd hung the moon. She wished she understood his motives, but she didn't.

He wanted something from her, but what? Her land? Her cattle? The money she'd get from the sale? He was different from the townspeople. No one had ever looked at her with respect before...except Granny.

Never a man. Somehow the look was different in his eyes. It frightened her and made her want to escape and yet run to it all at the same time. She despised these conflicting thoughts and feelings. She liked things orderly. Austin Sinclair was like a whirlwind spinning toward her, hell-bent on disruption. Her best choice was to outrun him.

"I was trespassing, Doc," Austin confirmed.

"I know that, son. I put that in my report."

"You did?" Monica and Austin replied in unison again.

Doc scratched his head. "Sure did. Which tells me the source of the rumors is not Sheriff Yates, but..."

"Roxy!" Monica replied with a snap of her fingers.

"That'd be my guess, yes." Doc nodded.

Austin's brows knitted. "Who's Roxy?"

"The biggest gossip in town," Doc replied. "Confidentially, she's the bane of everyone's existence. She hasn't got a life of her own, and so all she does is meddle."

Austin slid off the table, momentarily forgetting he was wearing nothing but his briefs and shirt. "I'll talk to her for you, Monica."

"I can take care of this by myself," she snapped. "I don't need any outsider—"

"Outsider?" Austin cut her off righteously. "The way I see it, I'm the victim here, not you."

She pointed to his leg. "Mister, you're more loco than everyone thinks I am!"

"How do you think it makes me look to my new neighbors that I was shot by a woman?" He growled back.

"Like a fool."

"You got that right, and I don't like it. If I decide I want to take matters into my own hands I'll damn well do it."

"Fine," she shouted, and glared back at him as fiercely as he was staring at her.

It was Doc laughing at them that dispelled the tension and anger in the room. "Wheeee-weeee!" he whistled. "I haven't seen that much fallout since Mount Saint Helens."

"Sorry, Doc," Monica said, and took a deep breath. In a calmer voice she asked Austin, "What can you say to Roxy that would help? The damage has been done."

"Don't be so sure. Being the victim, I could go to the sheriff and complain about the slander and libel I've been hearing about myself, and say that I know for a fact the source is coming from his office. He might put pressure on her and she just might shut up."

Doc smiled. "No one's ever done anything like that to Roxy."

"Are you serious?"

"Very," Doc replied.

"Then you're as much to blame as Roxy for not stopping her long ago."

"Probably so," Doc agreed with a nonchalant shrug. "But there's never been any real harm. Nothing much ever happens in Silver Spur. Till now."

Austin looked back at Monica. "You might think about letting someone help you out from time to time."

She felt as if her face were on fire, but she couldn't tell if she felt shame or anger. Then she realized she was feeling something altogether quite different. And it wasn't coming from her face, but a lower source. She wanted to look away, but couldn't. She hated the way he made her knees turn to water. She hated feeling vulnerable, and it was Austin's fault she felt this way. Being around Austin was just about the most unsettling thing she'd ever done.

"I'm going," she announced.

Austin couldn't get over the way she looked at him. He could see the pulse in her neck making her look like a she-wolf ready to pounce. Maybe she was as crazy as the townspeople said. Maybe he should watch himself more carefully around her like she'd warned him to. Maybe he should put his pants on....

Austin turned away from her, breaking the mood, and picked up his jeans and stepped into them. With the jeans halfway up his legs, he glanced at Monica and saw she was watching him closely. Very closely.

He turned away from her, not for modesty's sake, but because he didn't want her to see the satisfied smile he felt on his lips. He'd been right as rain. She wanted him.

Pointing at Austin, Monica cautioned, "You'd be best off if you stick to your own land and mind your own business." She practically bolted out of the examination room, down the hall and out the front door.

Austin turned to Doc. "Is she always so tough?"

"Yep."

"No wonder everyone thinks she's crazy. Does she always pick fights like that?"

"Most times."

"A man would have to be half-nuts to want to tangle with a mountain cat like her."

"Yep. Half at least."

Austin zipped his fly. "Just for the record, I've had my share of wacko women. I moved up here to de-stress and get away from nut cases. Believe me, you won't have to remind me to steer clear of her."

"I wouldn't dream of it," Doc said, chuckling to himself as he saw Austin out the door.

Five

Monica found Jake Simmons still at the barbershop, seeming to have no intention of leaving his cronies. They were gathered around him like mindless quail in need of a leader. Being a very large man in both height and girth, Jake used these attributes to subtly demean everyone else in his sphere. Jake was a jokester who found comedy in others' mishaps and shortcomings. Monica thought him a mean man, greedy and self-centered. Every time she had to deal with him she felt as if she were bargaining with the devil. However, in Silver Spur, Jake was her only connection to get her cattle to market.

Jake owned the holding pens, knew the Department of Agriculture examiners and paid his rail rental a year in advance. He paid Monica in cold cash, always telling her she was "making a good deal." Because she had no way of knowing otherwise, Monica believed him. Jake Simmons was also the richest man in town.

The ninety-two-year-old barbershop smelled of rum spice

tonic and cheap antiseptic used to clean combs and scissors when Monica walked in. Wooden chairs rimmed the room, and each was filled with Silver Spur inhabitants. The morning sun cut through the venetian blinds, illuminating blue clouds of cigar smoke, dust motes and airborne hair clippings. A funny, buzzing sound underscored the men's laughter as the barber shaved the back of Jake's neck.

Jake filled the black leather and chrome barber chair, his huge booted feet planted on the floor rather than the footrest which was too short for him. His thick mass of salt-and-pepper hair waved over his broad forehead. Deep furrows in his brow and around his dark eyes attested to his days on horseback, conjuring images in Monica's mind of cowboys of yesteryear. But when she opened the glass door and Jake frowned at her, she reminded herself there was nothing romantic or nostalgic about Jake Simmons.

"This ain't the beauty parlor, Monica. Or did you come here aiming to shoot up the rest of Silver Spur?" Jake howled.

The cronies sitting in the wooden chairs cackled, their voices sounding like magpies.

She ignored them. "I can go back and get my shotgun if you'd like, Jake. Or we can do business. What'll it be?"

Cocking his bushy eyebrow appreciatively, Jake replied, "Is it that time of year already, Monica?"

"It is."

His eyes fell from her face and slithered down her body slowly, as if he were memorizing every curve. She'd never had a man look at her this way. In high school, she'd always been scrawny and the butt of jokes. Due to her preoccupation with caring for the ranch and Granny over the past year, she hadn't paid much attention to the changes her body was making, now that she was out of her teens. Her clothes had always hung on her, until this spring. She'd thought her jeans and shirts had shrunk from using a new detergent she'd bought at the general store. She realized her dilemma wasn't going to be solved by going back to her old brand.

Jake's look made her feel slimy, and though it took some doing, she didn't flinch. She couldn't help thinking his eyes oiled their way over her, oozing venom in their wake. She refused to react to him, and hid her feelings the way she'd always done when she was threatened. Her eyes were placid, unperturbed when he finished his perusal.

"You've grown up...and out since I last saw you, Monica."

"How's your wife, Jake?"

The cronies cackled again, but quickly realized their mistake in taking sides against Jake. They stopped abruptly.

Jake pushed the barber away with his hand. "That'll be all." He waited patiently while the barber removed the cape and dusted off his neck. "I was sorry to hear about Adelaide."

"Thank you."

"I suppose that means you don't have any instructions from her this year."

"No."

"Too bad. She was always a shrewd businesswoman. Frankly, I don't know how she did it. Always knowing exactly how high to push me. How'd she do that, Monica, not having a telephone or television to keep up with the markets?" He winked at one of the cronies. "Magic?"

Monica realized he was setting her up again. The problem was that she needed Jake to buy her cattle. If she let him needle her a bit here and there to get the deal, the only thing that would be hurt was her pride. She'd had plenty of practice licking her wounds. "Maybe she was smart enough to read a newspaper."

Jake waved his hand dismissively through the air. "Yesterday's postings. Adelaide was a wizard. Come on, you can tell us, Monica. Was she touched? Or just plain loco...like you?"

The cronies burst into a round of cackling that could be

heard out on the street. Several bystanders turned toward the open door to the barbershop. The mailman left his route and walked across the street to join in the fun.

To Austin Sinclair, Silver Spur was much the same as the rest of the small Montana mountain towns he'd visited in his search for paradise. There were no chain stores here, not even a national grocery store, just the movie house, post office, a general store, a diner, one gas station, two churches, a combination Laundromat and dry cleaners, one clothing store, six bars and a barbershop adjacent to a beauty shop. The main street accommodated only three stop signs, and the parking was angled to the sides of the street making room for more pickup trucks than cars. There were no parking lots, no fast-food restaurants and no malls for people to congregate. Though the bars were active at night, in the mornings the action happened elsewhere.

When Austin left Doc's house, he went to the post office to check his mail, and on the way back, he heard the raucous laughter coming from the barbershop. One glance at the lithe blond woman standing in the doorway told him Monica was in trouble.

Mind your own business.

He could hear the warning echoing in his head. He knew better than to walk across the street. He was only asking for trouble if he butted in. After his encounter with the beautiful but decidedly tempestuous Miss Skye this morning at the doctor's office, Austin knew damn well his best course was to let sleeping dogs lie. People up here were wiser than he'd ever been. They kept to themselves and never told family business to anyone for fear of gossip. The fact that the Harrisons didn't tell Doc or Monica they were moving should have been a warning to him to keep moving down the sidewalk to his new Chevy Tahoe truck. But did Austin listen to the sound of reason? No, he didn't.

* * *

"Don't tell me she used the Internet," Jake prodded, still keeping his own laughter in check.

"The inter-what?" Monica was perplexed.

The magpies laugher was enhanced by the group outside the barbershop who'd flocked together. "She doesn't know what the Internet is," one woman squealed to an older woman next to her.

"Who doesn't?" a teenage boy asked.

"That young woman there," a middle-aged man said.

Austin walked up at that moment and elbowed his way through the people. He stood behind Monica in the doorway, the morning sun at his back. "Excuse me, I was wondering if you had time for a haircut?" he asked, looking pointedly at the barber and ignoring everyone around him.

The barber nodded. "Sure."

"Excuse me, Miss Skye," he said bowing slightly. "How are you today?"

The laugher died in an instant as they watched the stranger whom they all knew Monica Skye had tried to kill the night before.

"I-I'm fine."

"You're looking lovely today. Beautiful, in fact." Austin approached the barber's empty chair, nodded a greeting to the enormous man seated next to him. Austin stuck out his hand to the man. "I'm Austin Sinclair. Glad to know you. And you are?"

"Jake Simmons." Jake shook Austin's hand.

Austin sat in the chair and let the barber drape a white cloth around his neck. "You know, Mr. Simmons, I haven't lived here but a few weeks, and I must say that you people are very fortunate."

"How's that, Mr. Sinclair?" Jake asked.

Austin looked back to Monica and beamed widely. "Not only is the land breathtaking, but so are your women."

Gasps flew from the cronies' mouths. The laughter from the sidewalk died instantly.

Jake followed Austin's appreciative stare. "Monica?"

"Miss Skye," Austin said respectfully.

"But...but she shot you."

"And with good reason," Austin began and noticed every eye in the room and outside, including Monica's were pan-sized. "I was trespassing."

Dumbfounded, Jake demanded, "That's no reason to up and shoot someone...even a stranger. Everybody knows Monica always been a bit—" He tapped his temple.

"Frankly, I'd say she was nothing of the kind. I think she was simply being smart. Most women I know back in Chicago have guns under their beds in case of intruders. There are gun coaches tell them to shoot first and ask questions later. The statistics for assault and battery are staggering. Frankly, I told Miss Skye this morning while we were chatting over at Doc Kilroy's office, that her biggest problem was that she was not adequately armed. Buckshot is no way to deal with intruders." He turned back to Monica. "Isn't that right, Miss Skye?"

Monica couldn't believe her ears. No one had ever stepped up on her behalf that she could ever remember. And certainly never to Jake Simmons. Her first instinct was to ask Austin what the hell he thought he was doing. Instead she replied, "Yes, you suggested I buy a modern gun. Something more powerful like a Magnum, I think it was."

"Well, yes. Though I prefer a Glock myself." Austin turned back to Jake. "What do you like?"

Jake was speechless and the crowd knew it. They turned their attention back to the young man in the barber chair, wait-ing for him to assume the throne Jake had lost through default.

"Just a trim," Austin said to the barber who began clipping away.

The flock outside the barbershop realized the drama was over and fluttered away. The cronies picked up battered fishing magazines and buried their faces, cranking their ears so as not to miss a single word.

Jake bolted out of his chair, slammed a five-dollar bill on the counter and turned to Monica. "Let's go to my office to discuss this," he said.

"Discuss what?" Austin cut in. "If you don't mind my asking, Miss Skye?"

"Cattle," she replied quickly. "Jake buys everyone's cattle around here.

"Really?" Austin smiled benevolently at Jake. "What's it going for? Per pound on the hoof?"

"Forty cents," Jake answered swiftly.

"Forty?" Monica asked. "But I got nearly fifty last year. What's going on?"

Austin remained silent while Jake explained.

"Beef has been plummeting for years, Monica. I've been trying to tell you it's not like the old days. Every year it gets worse, and every year your grandmother insisted upon you putting all your profit back into the herd. Hell, if it weren't for me forcing her to buy those sheep a few years back, you wouldn't have any diversification at all."

"Yes, and there's no market for them, either."

"It takes time, Monica. You know that," Jake said. "Times are changing. People in the cities are eating more chicken and fish. Hell, even pork bellies are up to seventy cents. All of which means that beef is down."

Deflated and more than just a little worried, Monica said, "Well, I suppose if that's the best I can get…"

Raising his forefinger in the air, Austin interrupted, "I hope you don't mind my barging in here like this, but I happen to know a bit about the commodities markets. May I suggest, Miss Sinclair, that you think this offer over and get back with Mr. Simmons in a few days?"

"What for?" Jake demanded. "That's my offer. Period."

"I feel it wise that Miss Skye investigate her options first."

"Options?" Monica asked.

Austin straightened in the barber chair, keeping a simpleton's smile on his face for Jake's benefit. For his ploy to work, he would have to sharpen his poker skills. "When I was trespassing on Miss Skye's land I noticed that she had quite a few calves."

"She did?" Jake's interest was piqued. "You didn't tell me that."

Knitting her brows, Monica asked, "What have my calves to do with anything?"

Jake smiled smugly. "Veal. I'll pay fifty-four on the hoof for veal."

Austin didn't dare let Monica respond. "She'll consider the offer and get back to you. Won't you, Miss Skye?"

"But that would mean I'd have to come back to town," she said, wondering how many more trips the dilapidated truck could make.

"Precisely, Miss Skye," Austin gave her a commanding look.

She didn't know what he was up to, and she didn't like the way he took over her negotiations with Jake, but her inner voice guided her. "I'll get back to you in a few days."

Jake held out his hand to her. "I'll wait to hear from you, then," he said.

Monica stepped out of the doorway and allowed Jake to pass. She hadn't the slightest idea what had happened that morning but one thing was certain, Jake Simmons spoke to her in a way she'd never heard him talk before. She swore she heard respect in his voice.

"How do you like my haircut?" Austin smiled winningly and handed the barber five dollars.

"Why did you do that?" Monica asked.

"It was scraggly," he joked, while the barber took off the cape.

"You know very well I meant about Jake. This is my business deal, and I—"

Austin leaped out of the barber chair, crossed the room, grabbed her elbow and practically shoved her outside. "I highly suggest that if you don't want an entirely new set of rumors floating around town about yourself, it would be best to keep your mouth shut in front of those men in there."

Does he have to be right again?

"Let's go over to my truck," he said showing her the way toward his Tahoe. Hitting the remote control to unlock the doors, he said, "Get in."

"How did you do that?" she asked poking her head into the interior. "And what kind of seats are these?"

"Leather."

"This isn't leather. My truck has leather seats."

Austin rolled his eyes. "Just get in. We can talk, and no one will hear us."

"I don't care what other people—"

Interrupting her he said, "Who said anything about you? We're discussing business here."

"Uh, yes. Right."

"Get in."

Monica did as she was instructed and closed the door. Austin turned on the engine and set the digital temperature gauge to a comfortable sixty-eight degrees. "What kind of truck is this? There's no flatbed, and what's all this stuff?" she asked pointing to the computerized dash.

"You're right. It's a four-wheel-drive vehicle. Can I ask you something and you won't get angry with me?"

"It depends."

"Are you always so antagonistic?"

"I didn't know that I was."

"All I want to know is how long it's been since you've been in a new car?"

She shook her head. "I haven't." Crossing her arms over

her chest, she said, "I'm getting new tires, once I make this sale."

"I see." He watched her eyes as they flitted around the interior. He couldn't tell if he was seeing wonder or fear. Or envy. "That's the tape deck."

"I know what it is. Jill Gregory had a portable one in high school she used to play in study hall. Hers had earphones."

"Do you want me to play a tape? I've got a collection here in the glove box," he said, reaching across her to open the latch. He smelled it again, that unusual scent of wildflowers and vanilla she wore. He didn't think she would spend money on something as extravagant as cologne. Perhaps it was the soap she used or the shampoo, since the fragrance surrounded her like a veil.

"The kids in school used to play Bonnie Raitt. I liked her."

"I should have guessed you'd be a country-western fan," he said closing the door. "All I have is jazz and blues."

Her face brightened. "That's what Granny used to play. Do you have Bessie Smith?"

"Yeah, right." He stopped mid-motion. "More important, do you?"

"Sure. I told you, Granny played them...on her Victrola."

"Originals? Seventy-eights?"

"Yes," she replied flatly. "Hundreds of them. What I want to know is...what are we going to do about my herd?"

This is unbelievable, Austin thought. This woman has a fortune in antique records, and she's worried about making a few dollars on some cattle. She's not crazy—just uninformed.

"My impression of Jake is that he's not a reputable businessman."

"He's slicker than oil, is what he is," she said.

Smiling, he continued. "At least we both agree about what we're dealing with here."

"'We'? These are my cattle."

"Hear me out. I think Jake is taking advantage of you. I

think it's possible he's not quoting you correct prices. Maybe you should double-check the going rate."

"The radio Granny always used to listen to for the farm and market reports is broken. I'll buy a newspaper."

Austin shook his head. "Jake was right, that was yesterday's news, and we need the latest scuttlebutt. I'll call my old firm in Chicago, get some projections. Besides, calves aren't normally listed in the newspaper, but I could look them up for you on the Internet."

Monica frowned. "What is that exactly?"

Austin rolled his eyes. He was beginning to understand that Monica lived in an old-fashioned world and yet had enough exposure to modern conveniences to know what they were but not how they worked. And she owned damn few of them. Trying to explain computerized telecommunications to her would take a lifetime. "It's on my computer," he replied.

"Well, why didn't you say that in the first place?"

"What do you know about computers?"

"The administration office in high school had one. I don't know how to work one, but I've seen them. They're very expensive."

"Yes, they are."

"I have a typewriter. A Royal. It needs a new ribbon," she said halfheartedly.

"Probably a first edition," he mumbled to himself. "Well, let me know if you'd like me to get those prices for you."

"Is it a lot of work?" she asked.

"No."

Placing her hand on the smooth chrome door handle, she turned to him. "It would help me a lot. I could come to your house later this afternoon."

"That's fine," he replied.

She opened the door and got out. Just before closing it, she peered at him. "Why are you doing this, Austin? Being so friendly to me when I shot you last night?"

"I don't like to see people being taken advantage of," he replied honestly.

Monica's eyes held his for a long moment. She wanted to believe him, but every time she looked in his eyes, she was too aware of his maleness. She could hear her mother's voice talking to Granny one night after they thought Monica had been asleep for hours.

"Men always say things they don't mean. They do things they don't mean. And the thing I hate and despise the most is the subtle way they ease themselves into your heart like they were smoke under a doorsill. They make you think they're the most precious things in the world, and then they leave. Leave us women holding the bag. And their babies."

Granny's voice was softer, but filled with equal pain. "You love Monica as much as I love you, Rose. I wouldn't trade the world for either of you. Sometimes I think fathering our children is the only real purpose a man serves on this earth, and the tragic part about it is that deep down, they know it, too. That's why they fight us so hard for control. They have to be the breadwinners. Control the money. Control their jobs, their friends, wives and children. They wage wars to remind themselves of the awesomeness of their powers. But the truth is, they have none. We are the creators, Rose. We bear life and give life."

"That's right, Mama. We don't need anybody."

Monica heard Austin's voice invade her memories.

"Jake Simmons would take you to the cleaners, given half a chance. I'd love to see him get shot down."

Shot down? Like war? To prove your *might? Or mine? Is your offer to help me? Or yourself, Austin?*

Austin was smiling at her. "I'll see you later," he said.

She closed the Tahoe door. "Maybe," she said, and he drove away.

Six

Monica wanted to do it on her own. It was important that she not rely on Austin, and that was why she took the Philco radio apart. She could do this. She'd seen Granny work on the machine before, using a Phillips screwdriver, but no matter how much she jiggled the tubes and unplugged the fuses and put them back in, the radio did not work, and she wanted to hear the farm report.

She tossed the screwdriver into the toolbox. "Damn! Now, I'll have to go see him."

Walking to the large plate-glass window that looked out over the back of their property where the trees and grasses met the edge of a small lake, Monica forced herself to think of yet another memory about Granny. Anything, so she wouldn't think about Austin Sinclair.

The sun had passed behind the mountains, casting the gold-silver glow of twilight over the water and trees. How could it be possible that she'd shot Austin only twenty-four hours ago?

In that short span of time, he'd managed to stir a strange force inside her. He'd mucked up all her thinking processes. She found herself seeing the vision of his face wherever she looked, and the very worst part was that she wanted desperately to see him right now, even though she knew it was the worst decision she could make.

"I won't go." She chewed her lower lip anxiously and hugged herself. "I'll go into town tomorrow and make my deal with Jake, but I'll demand twenty-five cents a pound more. Maybe we'll settle at fifteen. And that will be that."

Once the deal was finished, there would be no more reason to see Austin. He'd stay on his property, and she'd continue with her life just as it had always been.

She leaned against the wide window frame just as she'd done nearly every evening of her life. She loved this view, especially at this time of night. When she was a child she thought she'd seen fairies dance among the wildflowers. Her mother told her fairies weren't real. She believed her. But sometimes when the last of the sunglow met the dawning of moonglow it still seemed to Monica that the earth seemed to come alive as if there magic in the air.

She opened the back door, walked down the wooden steps and through blankets of fragrant pine needles toward the water. Tawny-colored sunbeams split into a rainbow of colors across the lake. Monica reached out for them and then giggled over her foolishness.

Then it struck her. Child's play wasn't fun anymore. She could no more go back to the way she was yesterday than she could bring Granny back. Her world was changing, whether she liked it or not. She didn't like feeling defenseless against this inexplicable power that drew her or forced her to Austin. If only she could discern if he were the creator of that magnetism or was it something inside her? Perhaps it was outside them both.

Did he feel it? She'd seen nothing in his eyes or behavior

to think his insides were turning upside down. He was the one who'd seen her completely naked. According to her mother's tales, Austin should have been a raging beast wanting to mate with her. Though she was well-aware of the mechanics of sex, living on a ranch as she did, until she'd seen Austin today, she had not experienced passion. And surely, that must be what this hunger buried deep in her belly was called.

Because she'd been an outcast in school, Monica had never had the companionship of other girls or boys. She'd had no one to joke with. No one with whom to explore the universe of human sexuality. Monica was more than a virgin. She'd never even been kissed.

Leaning over the water's edge she stared at her reflection in the golden light. Suddenly she saw Austin's face next to hers. Her eyes were filled with desire, but his were not.

What would it be like to have you want me? she wondered.

Mesmerized by the vision, slowly Monica unbuttoned her shirt and let it fall to the ground. She dipped her hand into the cold water, then trickled it down the back of her neck. Another scoop helped to cool the fire in her heart. Still, she kept her eyes focused on the vision of his face. Cupping her breast with one hand, she held it out to him as an offering, but the vision did not change. She poured a handful of water over her full breast and watched the nipple harden.

Would it be like this if you touched me, Austin?

Monica had never experienced her sexual nature before. Much of it frightened her. Some of it did not. Mostly she was filled with curiosity. If Rose were alive, she'd explain that the nature of entrapment began with a woman's desires. She was responsible for the weaknesses inside her. She was to blame for "giving in" to a man. She was at fault for the wanting.

Monica slipped her hand into the water hoping to dispel Austin's face, but he stared back at her tenaciously. Trickling the water over her flesh, she let the rivulets course down her rib cage to her belly. She held her breath, the urges she experienced were so strong.

She would not see Austin tonight. Or any other night. Not until she tamed this wild animal inside her.

To put finality to her plan and staunch her own heat, she dunked her long hair in the cold water. Shivering, she put her shirt around her shoulders and raced back toward the cabin.

As she padded through the pine needles, she couldn't help thinking how incredibly intriguing it was that none of these sensations had occurred until she'd met Austin Sinclair.

Common sense told her he had nothing to do with her womanly awakening, but her heart told her something altogether different.

Monica's plan worked for two days. She and Daisy tended her regular chores and took a final count of both her cattle and calves. To keep herself occupied she'd risked taking the truck to town. Though it rattled and coughed as always, it was still in one piece when she parked in front of Highstatler's Pharmacy, the only newsstand in town.

Monica's intention was to buy the paper and leave before Bill Highstatler saw her. As much as she didn't like Jake Simmons, she liked Bill even less. He gave her the willies, plain and simple. Ever since middle school she'd never been able to figure out what there was about him, but he reminded her of a dark shadow in the woods; always lurking. He'd never done or said anything worse than anyone else in town. In fact, she didn't remember him ever being outright rude, as Jake had been the day before. But Bill had a mysterious side to him that made her wary, though she hadn't the slightest idea about what. She'd always made a point of staying as far away from him as possible.

The English Tudor-style pharmacy had been built during the twenties when most of the original town buildings had come into being. Silver Spur had been a mecca for wealthy

Californians back then like her grandfather. And like him, they'd left, too.

Inside the leaded-glass door to the right was the prescription counter where Bill's father, Vernon, worked. Dark wood shelves held a maze of toiletries, vitamins and personal hygiene goods in the center of the building and to the left was the soda fountain. Unfortunately for Monica, the newsstand was located at the rear of the store, making it necessary for her to pass the fountain where Bill was standing.

"Hi, Monica," he said pouring out a milkshake for the little boy and his mother who were seated atop chrome stools at the white marble counter.

"Hi," she replied, and kept walking rapidly.

Perched at the far end of the counter were two young girls about seventeen, Monica guessed. Whispering to each other, the blond-haired one signaled to Bill. "We've decided on the caramel nut sundae. Two spoons please."

"In a minute," Bill replied, his attention clearly still on Monica.

Casting a sidelong glance at the girls, Monica was aware of the petulant look they gave her. Smiling to herself, she wished she could tell the girls that their crushes on Bill Highstatler were in no jeopardy from her.

Bill sauntered to the end of the counter, tossing a white linen towel over his shoulder. "I'm surprised to see you, since you were in town yesterday. What's up?"

"Just getting a paper," she said quickly grabbing a copy of the Helena paper. "No *Journal?*"

He shook his head. "We quit carrying them. Folks don't seem to be much interested in the stock market anymore."

Pretending to read the headlines, she commented, "Makes sense. Ever since the crash, I suppose that would be the case."

"Which crash would that be," Bill asked, "1929 or 1987?"

Monica's eyes shot up. "Both," she said. "Amazing, folks just don't learn about being conned."

"Touché," he replied.

Monica felt the willies creeping up her spine. She quickly dug in her pocket and deposited a dollar on the counter.

Quick as a rattlesnake, Bill's hand covered hers. "I'll treat you to a chocolate soda."

Of all the sugary, dreamy concoctions in the world, Monica had long believed that nothing outclassed a bona fide chocolate soda made with fizzing seltzer water, the way they made them at Highstatler's. She'd had a soda at Ruth's Diner once. It was a falsehood of cheap ice cream, chocolate syrup and a clear soft drink. She'd hated it. Mrs. Vernon Highstatler was responsible for the homemade vanilla ice cream with chunks of vanilla bean and the homemade fudge syrup they used. Monica knew this because Granny had told her of all the things she would ever steal, it would be Mrs. Highstatler's fudge syrup recipe. When Monica was seven years old she'd made the fatal mistake of telling Billy Highstatler that his father's ice-cream sodas were her favorite treat, eclipsing Harriet Harrison's apple pie.

Bill had never forgotten it.

Monica eyed him suspiciously. He'd never offered her a free soda before. The offer was tempting.

The blond girl expelled a frustrated sigh, "Are you gonna make our sundae or what?"

Bill squeezed Monica's hand. Instantly she snatched it out of his grasp.

"What's the matter?" he said with a low laugh, but his eyes were filled with disdain.

"I've got to go. I've got a lot of work to do."

"Fine," he said. "I'm busy, too."

As Monica walked away, she overheard one of the girls saying, "Did you see that? I told you I was right. Bill's the cutest guy in town, and she turned him down. That girl is truly certifiable."

"Yep. She's crazy, all right."

* * *

Austin's crews put in two twelve-hour days back-to-back, and the progress they'd made was amazing. The new roof was completed, the skylights were mounted and the interior structure was ready for the plasterboard the following day.

He was proud of the new floor plan he'd created by opening up the living, dining and kitchen areas. Huge interior beams had been erected where the old ceiling and attic had been, and he'd faced the fireplace with floor-to-ceiling flagstone. The new flooring was pine as were the new kitchen cabinets. A granite countertop separated the kitchen from the dining area, which he would later surround with rustic wooden stools.

Today his old furniture had arrived from Chicago, and as he unloaded the black leather and chrome pieces, he was stunned at his earlier choice of decor. Depositing the sofa in front of the rugged fireplace, he realized his old life and his new one had little in common, other than the fact that he was a part of them.

After showering that night and warming a potpie in the microwave, Austin sat on his sofa looking up through the skylight at the stars. How odd it was that he'd never come to know himself until now. All those years living in the city, making mountains of money, had given him the ability to semiretire. He'd thought he would be able to give up the deal making, the thrill of the frenetic pace and the head rush of predicting winners. For the most part he'd been right.

"But only for the most part," he said as the scene at the barbershop came back to him.

There was no denying he'd overstepped his boundaries with Monica and jumped into the middle of her deal with Simmons. Instinct had provoked him to action. The need for closing the deal had excited him. The fact that Monica was being bilked had played a role, true. If the truth be told, Austin missed some things about his old life.

He missed his "guy time" with Brad and Steve. He missed

having a confidante with whom he'd discuss the day's deals. When he'd returned home after the encounter with Jake Simmons, Austin was expecting Monica to arrive that afternoon. But she never came. He'd wanted to talk to her about the deal like he used to do with his friends. He'd been pumped. Psyched. Wired.

Nothing happened.

She didn't show up the next day, either. Nor today. Austin could only guess she'd made the deal without his help.

Because of his deflated feelings, he began reviewing the wisdom of his choices. Perhaps his Chicago friends had been right that his breakup with Callie had cut him more deeply than he'd realized. He denied it vehemently then and even now; he knew that wasn't the case. But perhaps he hadn't truly been ready to leave the city after all. Maybe he should go back.

Running frustrated fingers through his hair, he said, "I can't be this messed up, can I? Surely I know what I'm doing."

He closed his eyes and opened them again. Through the skylight the stars looked as if they were falling in on him. Their light shone brighter, as if they were bringing him some eternal wisdom to clear his confusion.

Austin had never felt like this. He was a planner. An organizer. A doer. He didn't do anything by the seat of his pants, and yet he'd packed up his old life and left it in Chicago on a whim.

Was it a mindless, senseless act of sheer foolishness to come to Montana? What was out here for him, anyway? He'd plunged himself into his building project because the house hadn't suited him. It had been a fine home, well built, just antiquated. But he'd desperately needed to change it. He figured because he could afford it, it was his duty to change it. His thinking was no different from the contemporary mind-set of most of America.

Suddenly, however, he was part of Montana, and his thinking started to change, but in another direction. The people here had their ways and prejudices just like everyone else, but he found himself doing the craziest things. Such as coming to Monica's rescue like John Wayne. What was that all about? Why should he care about Doc? Or Jake? Or Monica? Who were they to him?

Too, he'd started viewing his old life as a film noir—joyless and dark. For nearly ten years he'd had clients for whom he'd invested hundreds of thousands of dollars; people he'd never met. They were voices over the phone. Orders on slips of paper. Files on his computer. They were networks through which he traveled on the road to success.

That was the kind of life that was familiar to Austin Sinclair. It was what he knew. It was what he did best. Now he'd stuck himself in the mountains with no links to his old world except the phone lines. The odd part was he wasn't picking up the phone to talk to any of them. He didn't want to talk to anyone but...Monica.

However, she didn't have a phone, and the fact that she hadn't come to him for his advice told him she'd meant it when she'd ordered him to butt out.

Feeling a twinge in his wounded leg, he admitted to himself that Monica wasn't going to change her mind about him or the fact that she wanted to be alone.

Shoving his fists in his jeans pockets, he walked outside and stood on the newly constructed, though unpainted, porch. He looked up the mountain to Monica's cabin far in the distance. He could see lights burning. Funny, it had been too dark the night he'd stumbled into her yard to notice that the cabin was two stories high and much larger than he'd thought.

"Looks like a party," he mused, though he doubted it were true.

A vision of Monica crossed his mind, and he found himself reliving every word they'd spoken, every look they'd exchanged. The very thought of her lit a glow inside him. He smiled. He laughed at her quirkiness and frowned over her rejection of him…of everyone. He wondered what it must be like to be a young girl, alone, living on a mountaintop, fearing nothing…except other humans.

"Perhaps we're more alike than we care to admit, Monica Skye."

Looking farther up the mountain, he saw the waning moon rise and crown the peak. "What the—" Peering closely, he saw a shadow moving along the ridge. Someone was pacing back and forth, the moon silhouetting their movements. A wind must have crossed the ridge, because he saw a skirt flutter around the person's legs. Then he knew.

"Monica."

The moment he uttered her name, the shadow stood still.

He felt it was as if she heard him. Then she disappeared into the night shadows.

She won't be passing by this way tonight.

He turned and entered the house hoping his obsession with the beautiful mountain woman would vanish once he fell asleep.

Seven

"Lord! I despise asking for help!" she growled, getting out of Granny's rocker so fast she nearly stepped on Daisy's tail.

The dog skittered out of Monica's way and followed her into the bedroom. Daisy hopped onto the huge four-poster bed covered in a wedding-ring quilt in soft pastel colors. Granny had made the quilt fifty years ago and had kept it in the cedar-lined closet upstairs along with stacks of other quilts she'd made during the long, bleak Montana winters.

Opening the closet door, Monica surveyed her collection of plaid shirts, both flannel and cotton and several pairs of jeans.

Stepping out of the jeans she'd gotten dirty this afternoon while cleaning out the horse stall in the barn, she plucked a clean pair off a hanger. She yanked the four-year-old jeans up her thighs and wiggled her hips into them. But they wouldn't zip.

"Hell's bells, Daisy, I don't know what's happening to me, but I'm getting big as a house. The waist is fine, but I could sure use at least another inch, two even, in the behind."

She wriggled out of the jeans and took out another equally old pair, but she had the same results. "Ugh! I've got to find something to wear."

Fifteen minutes later, Daisy was yawning and Monica was beside herself. "I can't wear any of these. And they're perfectly good pants." She held up the jeans for the dog to inspect.

Daisy panted appreciatively.

"Only one pair's been patched. How could I change so much in four years? Well, that tears it—once I get some money, I'm buying clothes that are two sizes bigger. That way, I won't be going through this again."

Stomping out of the room clad only in cotton underpants, she pounded up the stairs, flipping on lights as she went. Daisy was hot on her heels as they went to the seldom-used second floor where Monica's old bedroom was—the first of three on the left.

She turned on the Tiffany lamp, bathing the room in soft pink light as it filtered through the rose- and green-stained glass.

Daisy sprang onto the huge, white iron bed draped in white crocheted lace. The room was the antithesis of the masculine persona Monica displayed to the outside world. Here were her treasures. Here was her sanctuary, the place where she had dreamed about being an explorer to foreign lands when she was a child. A huge globe mounted on an iron stand and a telescope sat near the floor-to-ceiling window; the perfect instruments for mind travel.

The maple bookshelves installed when the cabin was built were filled with used books she'd bought at the annual book fair during the Silver Spur Harvest Festival every year. Sitting next to her high school textbooks were scores of first edition novels her grandparents had shipped from San Francisco in 1928. She'd reread her favorite historical biographies more than twice, wondering if she'd ever have the chance to be anything more than just Monica Skye.

From the closet Monica withdrew an aquamarine cotton dress she'd worn at her high school graduation. Its lines were simple with a scooped neck and short sleeves. She remembered the dress fitting loosely, since it had no defined waistline. Its only adornment were four pearl buttons at the bodice.

"Thank goodness Granny made this too big," she said to Daisy, who barked as Monica pulled the dress over her head.

She turned to the cherry wood cheval mirror and was horrified when she realized she could barely button the bodice. Her breasts seemed to overflow the neckline. "This looks awful."

She shoved herself down and pulled the neckline up which seemed to work, but the minute she moved her arms, she popped right back out. She inspected herself further and found the back of the dress hung over the crest of her rounded hips in a strange fashion.

"Becoming a woman isn't quite what I thought it was going to be, Daisy," she said dejectedly. "But this is all I have. So I guess it will have to do."

Rummaging in the closet further she found her white graduation flats. "Thank goodness my feet didn't get fat."

She turned out the upstairs lights and went back downstairs to the living room where she picked up the newspaper. She took a deep breath. "I can do this."

She thought of Austin. She remembered Jake's condescension. Her stomach roiled. She sank into the rocker. "I can't do this."

Daisy cocked her head to the left, then to the right as Monica rose again from the chair and began pacing.

Her resolve faded, then resurrected, then died again as she forced herself to follow through with an action that was foreign to her nature. She wrung her hands and paced. Having worked herself into a state of anxiety, she went outside to breathe the fresh air.

The night was incredibly clear and still. Spring had come early this year, and she could smell summer coming. The moon was huge as it hung above the cabin like her own dancing ball.

Monica had always taken it for granted how her surroundings were able to calm her inner storms, and tonight was no exception. She walked to the back of the cabin, smelling the pines. The lake looked like a silver mirror as she rounded it and headed up the trail to the top of the slope.

Standing up top, Monica looked down on her favorite view of Silver Spur. She could see the lights of the town twinkling like a tiny galaxy of stars come to earth. She liked being up here, distant from the people below, pretending she had power over them, instead of it being the other way around. Here, they couldn't hurt her. Here, she was safe.

As a child she'd pretended she was looking down on ancient cities in Egypt or China. She imagined how the people lived in their remote villages thousands of years ago. For a long time she wondered if they would have been more kindly to her. Then she'd learned to read in school and discovered that people like her had always been mistreated.

After all, a bastard was a bastard.

Monica had been in second grade the first time she'd ever heard the word *bastard* and Trace had been the one to say it. "My mama says I can't let you play jump rope with us," Trace had said.

"Why not? I'm better than you."

"Not 'cuz of that. 'Cuz you're a bastard."

"No, I'm not." Monica had replied, not knowing what she meant.

"Uh-huh. You are, too. Your mama didn't marry your daddy and so that makes you a bastard. Since your mama is dead, she can't never marry your daddy now. My mama says you can change a lot of things but a bastard is always a bastard.''

When Monica asked Granny for the truth, she confirmed what Trace had said. Granny had tried to be loving when she explained it, but the pain was searing. And it had never gone away.

Granny had held Monica while she cried. "You're much too young to understand this now, Monica, because Rose was so angry with your father after he left, but it wasn't always like that. When he was here, during that summer, she was different. She came alive like I'd never seen her. That's how I knew she was going to get hurt. Just like I did."

"She was filled with passion for Ted Martin. I tried to warn her, but she wouldn't listen. He was a poet, though an unemployed one. I told her he was a wastrel, but I gave him a job here, anyway. He fixed the roof that summer, mended fences and repaired all the things Rose and I hadn't had time, money or strength to do, in exchange for room and board. When he wasn't working, he was writing, he said."

"I knew he was seeing Rose. He said all the right things to win his way into her heart. I want you to always know that in that moment of time, when you were conceived, they loved each other. Rose had no anger in her heart then. But your father showed his true colors when he left the morning after Rose told him she was going to have you."

"He didn't want me?"

"I don't think it was that as much as he didn't want to grow up. Parenting is the most important job in the world. Your mother knew it. She wasn't afraid of it. She wanted you, just like I wanted to have Rose. In many ways your father was an angel. He brought you into our lives.''

"But I'm still a bastard."

"Only to those who don't have enough love in their hearts to see what a loving and beautiful girl you are."

* * *

Monica looked down on the Harrisons' old house where Austin lived. She saw the front door open and the figure of a man walk onto the porch. He was looking her way. She didn't have to wonder if he saw her. She knew he did.

There was something strange about the way she could think about him and only moments later he would appear. She wondered if that made him different from other people. There was no question in her mind that he was quite unusual. She'd never had anyone stand up for her like he did. No one in Silver Spur had ever had the guts to take on Jake Simmons, but Austin had.

Courage. That's what made Austin unique.

She could only hope she had equally as much.

Austin had gone to bed. Because his bedroom was not finished yet, he still camped out in the back room with his uninstalled microwave and computer equipment.

Wearing a University of Chicago T-shirt and boxer shorts, he'd punched his pillow, wrestled with the comforter and finally pinned the sheet trying to get comfortable. Snapping on the light, he decided that sleep was not forthcoming. His option was to watch television for another hour or read a book.

He padded into the living room where a stack of cardboard boxes held his collection of reading materials. Digging into the first box he found a stack of last year's *Forbes*. He took one of the magazines and was thumbing through it when he felt a chill cross the room.

He turned and saw his front door open. Startled, he dropped the magazine. "Monica?"

"You haven't fixed the door," she said, stepping inside.

"The door?"

"The lock rusted out years ago."

"Huh? Oh, yeah. The lock," he stammered. "I'd given up on you."

"Given up?"

"When you didn't come to see me, I figured you'd made your deal with Jake."

Shaking her head, she replied, "I haven't. I've been very busy at the ranch. Chores."

"I understand."

She walked farther into the room looking around at the changes. "What happened to the dining room? And the fireplace?"

He watched as she inspected the changes he'd made, still not quite sure if this was the same Monica Skye he'd met before. The dress she wore was alluring and did nothing to hide every curve of her body. He wondered if she was aware that her nipples showed through the tightly stretched cotton. He could tell she wore no slip, because the fabric seemed to wrap around her legs showing off the back of her hips. Her hair fell in thick, shimmering waves down her back and looked as if she'd spent hours brushing it. Though she wore no makeup, her cheeks were pink and glowing. But it was the softness in her eyes that drew his attention, as if she'd been crying. Even her voice had lost its cutting edge.

Had he been in Chicago and a girl showed up at his apartment dressed like a seductress, he would have known what to do. But this wasn't Chicago, and Monica Skye's favorite greeting card was a shotgun.

"If you don't like it, are you going to shoot me again?" he asked. When she spun to face him she was smiling.

"But I do like it."

"You're kidding?"

"No, it looks more like my cabin now."

"It does? How?"

"I have a ceiling like this and a similar fireplace. The main room and dining room are all in one, but the kitchen is separate. Even though my grandfather built it himself, he hired an architect of a friend of his. Mr. Morgan was his friend's name.''

"J. P. Morgan?''

"Yes,'' she replied and continued inspecting the kitchen where hollow places were marked with initials, DW, DO, S, and REF.

"Do you know who J. P. Morgan was?''

"Yes. Do you?'' Her eyes were glittering with mischief when she faced him again. "He built log cabins like mine in the Adirondacks and he made a lot of money.''

"That he did,'' Austin nodded and smiled back.

Monica's eyes scanned the room as if searching for something. Austin's shock over seeing this side of Monica finally dissipated. "Is there something in particular you were looking for? Something of the Harrisons', perhaps?'' Before she had a chance to jump into one of her tirades, he quickly volunteered, "I stored all their fixtures in the barn. If there's anything you'd want...something sentimental I mean, I'd be happy to—''

"Where's your computer?''

"My—'' He realized she'd come about the cattle deal. She hadn't dressed like this because she was attracted to him. She'd gone to all this trouble because she thought she'd have to seduce him to get the information from him. Her opinion of him was even lower than he'd thought.

"It's in my bedroom,'' he'd no sooner than said the words than he cringed. Was he laying his own trap for himself? "I'll go pull up the information and bring it out to you.''

She rounded the counter and walked toward him. As he felt his temperature rising, he couldn't help thinking she looked like a cool summer breeze gliding across his floor.

"I can't thank you enough for this,'' she said.

A pickup line if ever I've heard one. "No problem. I'll be right back. Have a seat on the sofa,'' he said, and darted out of the room.

Monica didn't know what was the matter with him just then. He'd looked like a scared jackrabbit. She sat on the sofa, leaned back, and when she did, she popped the top button of her dress. Hearing him stumble over something in the next room, she chuckled to herself and buttoned her dress.

It seemed strange to sit on this modern-looking leather sofa on brand-new wood floors and look at newly installed windows and unpainted walls. She'd expected to feel the ghosts of the past around her, but she didn't. Nor did she miss them the way she'd anticipated.

Instead she found herself liking this openness, the incredible mountain view from the wall of windows Austin had installed on the back of the house. She liked the strength in the massive stones that comprised the fireplace. It seemed appropriate that his furniture should be a blend of his old life and his new surroundings. She was stunned to find she felt at home in this place that was yet to be completed.

This time when she leaned back on the sofa and her top button popped she paid no attention, she was too busy looking at the stars through the skylight.

The experience was incredible to say the least. Why! It's like lying on a mountaintop, she thought. I know I'm inside, but I feel like I'm floating. How clever of him to think of this. Had he known to do this all along? What kind of man was this who needed to bring starlight to the indoors?

"Here you are," Austin said, exiting the back room and coming to a dead halt.

A shower of blond hair fell over the back of his black leather sofa as Monica stared up at the skylight. His eyes roamed over her beautiful face to the creamy swells of her very exposed breasts. She'd stretched her arms out along the top of the sofa looking like a goddess embracing her subjects.

"I like your window," she said sitting upright and facing him.

"Skylight," he corrected.

She looked at the sheet of paper he was holding out to her. "What did you find out?"

"We should push for seventy-five cents for the veal."

"You mean I should."

"Sorry."

She stood and frowned at him. "What are you trying to do, take over my business?"

"I'm not. It's just that this is what I used to do, and I guess I got a little carried away being reminded of the work."

Monica felt the hairs on the back of her neck prickle. Was he just like her grandfather? Had he come here thinking he wanted one thing and discovering he wanted another? "You liked it, then?"

"Yes," he said enthusiastically. "But too much of a good thing can kill you."

"Was it killing you?"

"In a way it was." He walked over to her and handed her the printout sheet. "Not that I'm ill. Actually, I'm healthy as a horse. I realized another five, ten years of that kind of stress and I'd be lucky to get away without serious health problems. It's common knowledge in my business that burnout is real and to be expected. The life expectancy of a trader is ten years, max. Only young men can take the pressure and stress. We're the ones with enough energy to handle it. We have to get in, make our mark, make our money and get out."

"What a terrible way to look at your life. Your work. What made you realize it was time you left?"

"Coming here...to Montana. I'd always been so busy rushing to grab that next sale. To beat the clock, get my orders in before the rally was over. Selling short. Selling long. My life was passing by me so fast I was out of breath. That first trip here, I had no idea places like this existed. I remember standing in my waders in the clearest, coldest damn water on planet earth, casting my fly, then casting again and again. I didn't particularly care if I caught anything. I just liked the feel of the sun on my face, the sound of the water rushing over the rocks behind me. I remember spending hours inhaling the air. I guess you could say I got drunk on this place. But the oddest part was when I went back to Chicago. Everything there seemed unfamiliar to me as if I didn't fit in. I realized I didn't anymore.''

"You left your heart out here," she surmised.

"Yes, I did," he said in a low voice, looking into her eyes. They were a clear blue rimmed in a velvety deep blue ring which made them intense and captivating. He had to remind himself that she'd come here to seduce him. She'd wanted something from him. Well, he'd given it to her.

So, why wasn't she leaving?

"I'm glad you've retrieved it, Austin," she said forcing herself to take her eyes off him. She'd gotten the information she needed. There was nothing else to say to him. She'd never have to see him again for anything. The best part was that she hadn't had to beg him to help her. He'd done her the favor automatically, as if doing favors for people was second nature to him.

Unfortunately, the power he used to make her move a step closer to him was more intense than what she'd experienced before. She wanted to breathe his breath, see through his eyes, taste with his tongue and feel with his hands. Looking at him, she felt her body come alive like it had by the lake yesterday, only this time the sensations were more pronounced.

Heat from the pit of her stomach spread like flashfire throughout her body. She could feel her breasts swelling and the place between her legs become moist.

"I have to go...now," she said.

Austin's erection had never been so strong, his blood pounding so forcefully he thought he'd explode. There was nothing he could do. It was best he get this over with. Then they could go back to their lives.

"Yes, you should...." Clamping his hand on her nape and pulling her into him, he kissed her.

Unprepared for his attack, Monica was stunned by the sensations she experienced. She felt like a rag doll in his arms, and she immediately regretted ever thinking he was not as muscular as the mountain men she knew. His arms were like steel as they crushed her breasts to his chest. She could feel the definition of his chest muscles against her soft flesh and through the thin fabrics they both wore. She slid her hand up his bare arm, marveling over the prickle of the hair on his forearm.

The musky smell of him was intoxicating as she breathed with him. He tasted of mint toothpaste and his own honeyed juices. It was a divine concoction laced with something she was certain was a narcotic because she knew she'd never get enough of him.

His lips were commanding yet gentle, but when his tongue forced her lips apart she was shocked again. Was it possible to make the incredible sublime? His tongue parried with hers, stroking her and slipping along the soft walls of her mouth. She felt chills race down her spine and up again, eliciting a low moan from deep inside.

She slid her hand around his nape, hoping he'd never let her go. Suddenly she realized this was the adventure she'd been wanting all her life. She was an explorer venturing into uncharted territories, and he was to be her guide. With every plunge of his tongue, she felt a tempest burning. Her breasts heaved against him, though not from breathing. She needed the caress of his body against her to create the exciting jolts that emanated from her nipples down to her loins.

Surprisingly she reveled in the sensation as he pressed himself against her. Her own pulse quickened and seemed to beat in rhythm with his, creating an ancient dance she was eager to learn.

A sound, low and hushed, came from his throat, thrilling

her. His hand was tighter on her nape as he turned her head and slanted his mouth over hers, forcing his tongue deeper, then deeper still. She thought she would faint from the joy of his onslaught.

Instead she felt massive rushes of electricity jolt through her, and just when she thought she couldn't stand the pleasure any more, his hand clamped over her breast. Her flesh overflowed his hand; her nipple resting between his forefinger and middle finger. Slowly, he tortured her by rubbing his fingers back and forth, making the nipple hard and sending searing bolts of indescribable intensity through her. She pressed herself into his hand, demanding more. Needing more.

Lustful pangs forced her legs wider apart.

"Monica…"

How was it possible that the sound of her own name, uttered so quietly and with such desperation, could make her knees turn watery?

Suddenly he tore his mouth from hers, and just as she was about to cry out over the loss, he devoured her breast. The friction from his tongue against her nipple was exquisite. All that had passed before was eclipsed in this single gesture, and she believed nothing more he could do could possibly be as exhilarating.

But she was wrong.

She hadn't felt him lift her skirt, nor had she felt his hand as it slipped down her panties and between her legs. The sensation was like picking up a live wire. She felt like jumping out of her skin, but she was too riveted to the spot to move. His fingers stroked her again and again, forcing moans and small cries from her.

"You want me?" he asked, lifting his head from her breast and looking into her opened eyes.

She blinked.

Austin abruptly stopped. "What am I doing?"

There was perspiration on his forehead, his skin was as

flushed as hers, she thought, when she finally regained her sight. She felt as if she'd been in a fog and had now come into the light.

She blinked again.

"I'm sorry, Monica. I got carried away."

"Carried away?"

"Yes, and it's all my fault."

"Your fault?"

He released her and began buttoning the bodice of her dress. She dropped her chin to watch what he was doing.

His voice was raspy when he spoke and filled with apology and something else, but she wasn't sure what. "I want you to know I didn't plan to... What I mean is...it won't happen again."

"It won't?"

"I can only hope you'll forgive me. Please, say you will."

"Yes, of course," she replied, coming to her senses.

He kept his arm around her waist as he walked her to the door. "Should I walk you back to your place? It's quite late and I—"

"No. I've known the way since I was a child."

"Of course," he said sheepishly.

She opened the door herself and walked through it. Her legs were moving, though she couldn't feel her muscles quite yet. She had no idea how long it would take for the sensation to return, if ever. Nor did she know how long it would take for her mind to begin to function as it once had. She supposed she would normalize again. Wouldn't she?

Or was this what had happened to her mother when she'd fallen in love with her father? Was this how she'd lost her heart and mind?

Passion. That's what this is.

The only thing was, Austin hadn't felt, too. He was in complete control of himself. He'd been able to talk, and he'd been the one to send her back home.

He'd apologized. And he'd said it would never happen again.

And thank God! She didn't think she could take a second time.

Eight

Word was all over town in less than an hour. Monica Skye had coerced Jake Simmons to pay her seventy-five cents a pound for her calves. It was the highest rate Jake had ever given a rancher. The fact that Monica Syke, "the mountain woman," had accomplished such a feat made the coup all the more intriguing.

The rumor mill rehashed and embellished the barbershop scenario to legendary proportions. The mayor, who owned the largest herd of cattle in the area, suggested the co-op hire Austin Sinclair to negotiate all their sales. The co-op members instantly announced a special meeting for the following night. Handbills were scribbled out, copied on the Highstatler's Pharmacy copier and nailed to telephone poles and put on car windshields before noon.

Walking out of Jake's office with the signed documents she'd demanded from Jake to close the deal, Monica found one of the handbills under the Ford's inoperative windshield wipers. Not knowing she was the inspiration behind the "special meeting," she placed the handbill along with the documents inside the truck and locked it.

Because Monica was used to the townspeople gawking and poking fun at her, she didn't react to the inordinate amount of attention she was getting that day as she went about her errands. Nor did she realize it was admiration in their eyes and not derision.

A woman under the drier at the beauty shop looked out the window, and upon seeing Monica crossing the street to the general store, said to the woman next to her, "Elma said that Trace Southern told her Jake nearly bust a blood vessel wanting Monica's calves so badly. Seems Monica was the only one in the valley with calves to sell."

"She's a pistol, that girl. Just like her grandmother," the other woman said.

By the time Monica arrived at the general store, Doc, who was there buying groceries, knew more of the details of her deal than she did.

Her jaw agape, Monica commented cryptically, "Trace works fast."

"Always has," Doc agreed. "She was on the phone blabbing to the beauty shop while she was typing up your papers. I heard it from Bill Highstatler when I was at the pharmacy. She called him next."

"Really? Why him?"

Doc eyed her suspiciously. "You don't know, do you?"

"Know what?"

"That Bill Highstatler's got a crush on you. Has since he was a kid."

She laughed out loud. "You've got to be kidding."

Doc peered at her, his eyebrows knit. "Sometimes I think Adelaide did you a disservice sheltering you like she did. Everybody in town knows how he watches you like a hawk when you come to town."

"That's because he hates me. Besides, I've never heard this malarkey from anyone else."

"Since when have you asked anyone about anything?"

"Huh?"

"You barely confide in me, let alone anyone else in town."

"That's true. It's best that way," she replied firmly.

"Maybe when Adelaide was alive it was all right for you to think that way, but your life is different now. Things are changing for you. I can tell."

Her eyes ballooned. She couldn't help wondering if he knew about Austin and what she'd done with him last night. "What can you tell?"

"That you're ready to be a woman. Get married maybe. Have children."

Shaking her head vehemently, she retorted, "You couldn't be further off the mark if you tried."

Doc looked down his nose at her. "What do you call those sparks between you and Austin Sinclair? And don't tell me buckshot."

"Austin Sinclair?" At the sound of his name she felt her skin heat up. She hoped to God she wasn't blushing, but she had the sinking feeling she was. "That's ridiculous. He's everything I loathe in a man. He's a stockbroker."

"Yes, and he's put a fire in your furnace."

"He's done nothing more than advise me about my sale, and that's all," she lied, looking Doc in the eye.

"Maybe you can fool other people, Monica, but I brought you into this world."

Expelling an exasperated sigh, Monica said, "Is there something else you'd like to talk about?"

"Yes, but I'd rather do it in my office."

"There's nothing we can't discuss right here and now."

"Yes, there is, Monica." He moved closer and whispered, "Did Adelaide ever discuss contraception with you?"

Monica thought her toes would curl with embarrassment. "I don't think that's a problem."

"I hope not," Doc replied, and walked to the counter to check out.

Both stunned and embarrassed, Monica grabbed a round box of oatmeal, and when she turned around she ran smack into Trace.

"Trace, I didn't see you!" Monica felt her blush quickly resurrect.

"I was just getting a power bar for my lunch," she replied, holding it up to show her.

Monica didn't miss the vicious gleam in Trace's eyes as the girl walked away. For as long as Monica had known her, Trace had always had a burr up her butt for Monica. Granny had told Monica that Trace was jealous of Monica, though she'd never believed it. Monica knew she wasn't a threat to Trace for any reason. She wasn't out to steal Trace's job or boyfriends. Trace's behavior didn't make any sense.

Austin spent two days at hard labor hoping to eradicate all thoughts of Monica from his brain. While the roofers finished reshingling the old roof, two carpenters finished framing in the area behind the kitchen that would become the new master suite. Austin floated and taped the plasterboard in the kitchen, and with the help of the cabinetmaker, set in the last of the kitchen cabinets and hung the doors. At night after the crews left, Austin painted the living room walls, hung wall sconces, adjusted ceiling mounted canister lights and ran stereo wires. Only at dawn did he allow himself an hour's sleep before the crews arrived again.

Suspended in the twilight between wake and sleep, Austin relived Monica's kisses. It was as if she'd come to him again, appearing in his doorway like a phantom, though there was nothing unreal about her touch. Having tasted the sweet wine of her lips and tongue, Austin felt intoxicated all over again.

Only, this time he didn't stop the kiss. She didn't break away. She reached for him and undressed him slowly, making certain she touched every inch of his body with her fingertips and lips. She lingered longest at his most sensitive spots, the hollow of his neck, the underside of his jaw, the crook of his elbow and the flatlands of his belly just below his navel where he only hoped she would travel lower. Delighting in the seductive moans he elicited from her, he was ready to explode.

"Monica!" he called her name urgently, and woke himself up.

He was covered in sweat. Raking his fingers through his hair, he groaned, "I'm making myself nuts."

He hauled himself out of bed and stumbled to the kitchen to make a pot of coffee.

"Mature men don't obsess about women. Certainly not me!"

Believing himself to be suffering from the aftereffects of career burnout, Austin reasoned that time and work would rectify his preoccupation with Monica.

Half a dozen pickup trucks pulled up to Austin's house. The sound of clanking tool belts, air compressors to run nail guns and paint sprayers sounded like a symphony to Austin. He was proud of the house he was building. He was prouder still of his own participation. Daily, he was learning that he not only had a talent for carpentry work, but that he enjoyed the work.

Walking up to Jess Techner, the crew boss, Austin said, "I think I'd like to try working on the roof today."

Shrugging his shoulders nonchalantly, Jess replied, "It's your money and your butt if you fall. Just remember I don't have accident insurance on you."

Austin laughed. "I think I can handle it," he said, and took the portable nail gun from Jess.

The sun rose brightly in the cloudless sky as Austin planted his feet firmly on the plywood and took instructions from Jess on how to overlap each shingle covering the previous row's nail heads.

The work fell into an easy rhythm for Austin, enough that Jess took one of his men off the roof and put him to work on the master suite addition. After an hour of nailing shingles, Austin heard a thunderous sound coming from above.

The sound grew like the mounting roar of a tidal wave as it gained strength and mass. "What the hell is that?" Austin asked Jess who had quickly walked up to the peak of the roof.

Smiling broadly, Jess pointed to the far side of the slope. "That sound is what Montana is all about," Jess said as Austin stood next to him.

"Cattle…" Austin said with a rush of awe.

Hearing a whistle and the repeated slash of rawhide as it whipped and snapped the air, Austin felt chills on the back of his neck. *Monica.* Though he couldn't see her, he sensed her presence.

Shading his eyes with his hand, he peered into the distance looking for her. Appearing in the midst of a brilliant sun ray, he saw her riding a magnificent chestnut stallion, her blond hair tied loosely and falling down her back. Sitting on her horse with the grace of a practiced equestrian, Austin watched as she called to her cattle, brandishing her whip overhead.

She was the most extraordinary sight he'd ever seen. She was prideful as she strutted her horse back and forth, keeping her cattle expertly in check. He wanted her more than before. Just taking her body wouldn't be enough. He had to have all of her.

"That's one hell of a woman," Jess said, admiration imbuing every word.

"She is that," Austin agreed unable to take his eyes away.

"And just about as loco as they come."

"Why do you say that?"

"Look over yonder. She's taking that herd in all by herself.

Her and that dog of hers. She hasn't ever hired any help that I know of."

"What's wrong with that?"

"Hell, it ain't neighborly is what. People in town need jobs. They've got families to feed. Bills to pay. Take yourself, for instance, you come up here and first thing you do…you hire my crews. Folks in town think you're a hero before you've moved in."

"I thought they were mad because I've—" he paused trying to remember Monica's words "—'desecrated' the Harrison house."

"Where in the hell did you get that notion? This whole valley needs renovation."

Austin looked back at Monica as she drove her cattle down the valley to where Jake's pens were located outside of town. "I would have liked to have done all the work myself, but I'm not that good," he said thinking of Monica's grandfather who built their cabin by himself. Maybe Monica would have admired him for that.

"Good thing for us you're not," Jess laughed. "Fact is, you're the first this valley's seen of real money since—" he looked off to the distance at Monica "—since Foster Skye hired the entire town back in '28."

Craning his neck around to stare at Jess, Austin said, "I was under the impression Foster built that cabin by himself."

"She tell you that?" Jess motioned his head in Monica's direction.

"Yes."

"In a manner of speaking, he did. Just like you're building this place. It's your money, isn't it?"

"But I—"

"Listen, Monica probably believes that story herself by now, she's told it so many times. Nobody's ever figured out why she lies so much."

Austin's eyes traveled back to Monica's diminishing form

as she entered the valley. "Building a house is a creative and enduring tangible. At least that's how I view it. Maybe in her mind, his building the house makes up for leaving her grandmother, whom she obviously loved."

Jess scratched the stubble on his cheek. "I never thought of it that way."

"It's a good way to see it," Austin replied and went back to his work.

The roof was finished before noon. Austin received a call from the hardware store that the kitchen cabinet hardware he had ordered had arrived. "I'll be there in an hour to pick it up," he told them.

While paying for the hardware, Austin couldn't help overhearing the townspeople conversing about Monica's cattle sale. Twice he heard his name mentioned, and though he was standing at the register in clear sight, he was not recognized. They talked about him as if he were some kind of hero. His immediate inclination was to protest. He was a broker. That was his expertise was all. But that wasn't how they saw it.

What disturbed him most was that every time he heard Monica's name mentioned, a twinge of excitement shot through him. He found himself craning his neck to hear more. Peppered throughout their story were thinly veiled slurs about Monica, albeit holdovers from the past, that caused an inordinate and inexplicable anger in him. He'd thought to leave well enough alone. But he couldn't. Wouldn't.

"Monica Skye has more integrity than any person I've met in Silver Spur," Austin said combatively to the middle-aged man who worked the plumbing aisle. "Not to mention she's the smartest businesswoman I've met in a long time. Coming from Chicago, a haven for bright, savvy and assertive entrepreneurs, I think Monica's got more balls and guts than anyone I've ever met."

"I wouldn't go that far," the man replied.

"Well, I would," Austin refuted, and left the building.

Taking a deep breath to clear his anger, Austin chastised himself for doing precisely what he'd struggled not to do. Obsess over Monica.

Walking toward Highstatler's, Austin found himself remembering how he felt holding Monica, kissing her, touching her, nearly taking her. Once again he thought he'd explode. He wanted her badly. Very badly.

Being brutally honest with himself, he had to admit he was drawn to her like a moth to a flame. He almost didn't care what the consequences would be. Being a conscientious man, he had to think things through and not allow his emotions to rule his behavior. He wasn't sure what was going on in his head, but there was no question, he was out of control. No matter how much he struggled with himself, his logic was not winning this battle. He had no choice but to be as realistic as humanly possible. He had to take precautions.

Walking into Highstatler's, Austin smiled at Trace, whom he'd met at the general store on his last trip to town. He knew the pretty girl worked for Jake Simmons, so he was guarded about what he said in relation to cattle, Monica and his participation with both.

"Hi, Austin," Trace cooed.

"Hi," he replied with a friendly, but not encouraging, smile. He didn't miss the flirtatious look she gave him. He pretended preoccupation with shopping. He picked up a bottle of shampoo.

"In town for the day?"

"Just a few errands."

"Yeah, I saw you coming out of the hardware store. How's everything at your house?"

"Fine," he read the label on a bottle of multivitamins.

"I hear it's like nothing else the valley's ever seen."

"Mmm." He nodded and looked around impatiently. "If you don't mind, Trace, I've got to get back to my crews.

Today's a really important day…joists going up and all. You understand.''

"Sure, Austin. Sure.'' She started to turn away and then said. "I saw Monica the other day at the general store.''

At the sound of her name, Austin's attention was piqued, and it was all he could do to remain unaffected. "Really.''

"Yeah, she was making an appointment with Doc.''

Thinking the comment strange, Austin didn't trust it. "I'm sure it's nothing.''

Folding her arms under her ample breasts and lifting them seductively, Trace replied, "I'm sure.''

Austin turned down the aisle and disappeared behind the paper goods. All Trace's sexual ploy had done was to remind him of Monica's sweetness. Visions of kissing Monica's breasts swept through his brain like a brush fire. Sweat erupted on his forehead. "God, I'm in serious trouble. Maybe I should be the one seeing Doc,'' he mumbled to himself.

Then he spied a rack of condoms. When he'd promised himself he would protect himself, he'd been thinking to cut himself off from Monica both mentally and physically.

Taking a box off the shelf he said to himself, "I have a feeling I'm going to need these.''

Nine

Monica cashed Jake Simmons's check at the bank and stuffed the money into her grandfather's leather valise. She'd used the valise for all her important papers and bank transactions just as Granny had said her grandfather had. Walking out of the bank with Daisy at her side, she found Austin standing at the parking meter where she tied her horse.

Austin smiled. "I thought I might find you here."

Clutching the valise tightly under her arm, Monica untied the horse's reins keeping her eyes away from Austin's face. She didn't trust herself this close to him. "Guess I was easy to spot, leaving Starshine here."

"That's his name?"

"Yeah, I named him myself."

"Romantic name."

She moved toward the saddle, which placed her closer to Austin. "I wouldn't know."

"I saw you earlier today coming down from the mountain," he began. "I was standing on my roof."

The admiration in his eyes was apparent, and for that she wanted to thank him, but she didn't dare. If she lingered too long, if she stood too close, she would want things from him she was better off not knowing. "On your roof? Did you get it finished?"

"Yes."

"That's good. Well, I've got to go," she replied, and placed her foot in the stirrup. Getting away from Austin was imperative.

He grabbed her waist. "Don't go...I wanted—" Instantly he dropped his hand.

His touch was like a brand. She reacted in the worst way possible. She turned to face him. "What?"

Touching Monica, looking into her eyes and being this close to her gave Austin the heady sensation he remembered feeling after four glasses of fine Bordeaux. "Come to dinner tonight. I'd like to cook for you."

"Why?"

"Because I'd like you to see what I've accomplished since you were there last."

"Is it so much?"

He laughed lightly. "Not really. I felt I needed an excuse to see you. The truth is, I'd like to spend some time with you to get to know you better. We are neighbors, you know."

Monica's eyes fell to his lips as he spoke. It was too easy to remember his kiss and the sublime pressure of his invading tongue. Even now his fingers crept slowly up her rib cage. She could feel him gently pulling her closer to him. Her head pounded with confusion as her resolve never to see him again battled with her desire. "I have plans tonight."

"Really?" He asked skeptically. "Another man?"

His joke tasted sour, reminding her of other taunts. "It's none of your business," she said angrily.

He averted his eyes, refusing to accept her rejection as permanent. "You're right. Perhaps some other time."

"Perhaps," she said coolly while internally hearing a nagging inner voice telling her to leave quickly. "C'mon, Daisy," she said as the dog pranced past Austin.

Austin stepped back as she mounted her horse, pulled the reins and trotted her horse down Main Street, Daisy keeping pace alongside her.

Monica had concluded her business. It had been a successful day. As she reached the edge of town she turned around, expecting to see Austin still watching her, but he was gone. Disappointment sat heavily on the corners of her mouth.

Austin barged into Doc's house unannounced. Myrna Paulson, Doc's nurse, was holding a three-month-old screaming baby, while the baby's mother was dressing after an examination.

"Where's Doc?" Austin asked Myrna.

She nodded her head toward the examination-room doors, where Doc was making a notation on a medical chart.

"Doc, I've got to see you," Austin bellowed, his face filled with anxiety.

"What's the matter, son?"

"It's Monica."

"Lord! Has she shot you again?"

"No, Doc, it's nothing like that."

The examination-room doors opened and the young woman stepped out. Austin sprinted into the room and waited for Doc, who lingered momentarily with Myrna.

"What's this all about?" Doc asked, coming in and closing the pocket doors.

Austin paced while he spoke, seemingly unaware of his peculiar behavior. "I think I've got the flu. It's some kind of bug."

"What are the symptoms?"

"Restlessness. There's a lot of that. I can't sleep. Never in my life have I not been able to fall asleep at the drop of a hat.

That's very weird for me. And loss of appetite. In fact, I don't remember the last time I've eaten. Yesterday I might have had some chips. I had an apple today. No, that was the day before.'' Slamming his hands on his skull he exclaimed, ''I can't remember. God! I've lost my mind. I need a CAT scan. Something in here is wacko,'' he tapped his temple. ''Must be my gray matter has turned to mush…evaporated. I need something.'' He threw his hands in the air. ''Maybe a Valium.'' He looked at Doc. ''What do you think?''

Doc bit his lip to keep from chuckling. ''I want you to go home and take a long, hot shower. Relax. Have a drink. A stiff one. That'll help more than pills. Sip it slow.''

Austin stared at Doc. ''That's it?''

''While you're at it, you might want to think about Monica.''

''Monica? What she got to do with my being sick?''

''I could be all wrong about this, and I have been known to be wrong before, though I don't recall those occasions offhand, but my guess is Monica has everything to do with it.''

''I'm that transparent?''

''Chances are.''

Austin shoved his hands into his jeans pockets. ''She doesn't want to see me.''

''That's a horse of a different color.''

''When she looks at me, I get the sinking feeling she's looking at her grandfather. One minute she venerates him, making me feel like I could never live up to her image of him and then next I feel her condemnation. I'm riding this emotional roller coaster, knowing I should get off but wanting to stay on no matter what the cost.'' He looked at Doc's concerned expression. ''I'm going nuts, aren't I?''

''I'd say so.''

''So what the hell do I do?''

Doc slapped Austin on the back affectionately. ''Go home and have that drink. The answer will come to you.''

Shaking his head, Austin replied, "I'd like to say you've helped me a lot, Doc, but I'd be lying."

Doc smiled. "I have to look after Mr. Haskins's bronchitis."

Austin's frustration faded. "I apologize, Doc. It's just that—"

"I know, son. You've never been in love before. Don't worry. It's not fatal."

"That's not true. I was almost married. It was a disaster. I swore I'd never get involved again."

Doc smiled. "If you were that deeply hurt, you wouldn't be having these problems with Monica."

"Why not?"

"Because you'd still be pining away for what's-her-name. You'd be thinking of ways to get her back. Monica wouldn't have a chance, if you were ever really in love with someone else."

"That's nonsense."

"Sorry, I've been around too long and figured out some things lots of folks can't see. That's why they call me Doc. Now, get on outta here. I'm busy."

Reluctantly Austin left the examination room. He wondered if Myrna could tell he was stumbling as he walked out the door.

In love? Was Doc crazy? He wasn't in love with Monica. Oh, he wanted her sexually. He lusted after her, but love? No way. He'd been in love before, and it had felt nothing like this. This was weird. This was a nutty possession. It was obsession. It was a treatable malady like other neuroses.

Austin knew his problem wasn't that he was in love. His problem was there was not a single psychiatrist in Silver Spur.

Monica rode Starshine at a thunderous pace back up the mountain and across the emerald grazing land her sheep kept groomed. Here she could tame the whirlwind inside her mind that Austin created every time she saw him. The out-of-doors had never failed to clear her head. This time she needed it to clear her heart.

Daisy bolted across the landscape, making her presence known to the flock. She barked and scampered across the thick, tall grass, making Monica smile as she inhaled the fresh air.

When Daisy's barking quieted, Monica heard a low, animal moan coming from a clump of trees. She'd heard the sound many times before and knew a new lamb was about to be born. Quietly approaching the scene on foot, Monica realized the mother was having a difficult time with the birth. Once before, Monica had delivered a calf in the breech position, and it was her guess this was the case for her sheep.

"Hold on, girl. We'll do this together. Everything will be okay," she said rolling up her sleeves.

Monica waited until the last contraction passed before inserting her hand into the birth canal. The sheep's painful cry echoed through the hills.

Despite his respect for Doc's wisdom, Austin knew a drink was not the answer to his problem. It was impossible for him to be reflective in the midst of electric saws, hammers and nail guns.

"Fishing is what I need," he decided, and grabbed his rod and reel.

The stream that fed Monica's lake began in the high country beyond her grazing land and pastures. It was a beautiful ride to the site, which Austin didn't mind at all. He rolled the windows down in the Tahoe and inhaled the clean air. With every tree he saw, every cloud, he believed he'd made the right decision coming to Montana. He was truly home. He stopped the truck for a moment and turned off the engine.

Smiling at the profusion of early-summer wildflowers, Austin heard a mournful cry. He heard it again. Suddenly realizing the sound came from the direction of Monica's pastureland where she kept her sheep, Austin turned the Tahoe around.

"Someone's in trouble," he said, driving the Tahoe off the road and over the field. Drawing closer to the sound, he saw Monica. At first he thought she'd been thrown from her horse, but then he realized she was bending over a sheep. Not wanting to startle either Monica, who still hadn't seen him, or the sheep, Austin pulled the Tahoe to a stop and ran the rest of the way.

"You need help?" he asked, rushing up to her.

Monica looked up at him as if he were crazy. "How many times have you helped give birth?"

"Twice."

"I'm surprised."

"Just dogs, though. No sheep."

"Hold her hind legs so I can get a better grip," Monica ordered urgently.

Dropping to his knees, Austin caressed the sheep's extended abdomen before gently taking hold of her legs. "Is it breech?"

"I'm afraid so," Monica replied. "I have to turn the baby, but I can't seem to—" She stopped suddenly, a horrified look on her face.

"What's the matter?"

"It's twins!"

"Both breech?" Austin asked.

"No wonder I wasn't getting anywhere. I had the wrong set of legs!"

"Some vet you are," he teased, watching Monica's eyes fill with concern. "You'll be fine," he assured her. "You better work fast, the mother is losing energy."

Monica turned the first baby around, pulled slowly and delivered a perfect lamb. "She's beautiful."

"Yes, she is," Austin smiled at the newborn as she unfurled herself, then tried to stand. "Here comes another contraction."

The sheep moaned deeply as the second lamb presented its head. Monica eased the baby lamb into the world. "Oh, boy!"

"One of each. A perfect family," Austin said watching brother and sister stumble over each other. "I've got some old towels under the front seat. I'll get them."

Using the torn terry-cloth towels emblazoned with a hotel logo, Monica and Austin cleaned the lambs and finally themselves.

Austin sat back on his knees watching as the lambs suckled their mother and she licked their heads affectionately. "Nature is a curious thing. If I were this mother I'd be wondering where the heck the father was. Shouldn't he be here helping out? I should think pacing in the waiting room would be the very least he could do," he joked.

Monica observed the sheep dourly, "She did just fine all by herself. As most females do."

"Especially you, right?"

His eyes were pointedly accusatory, and she wanted desperately to be indifferent, but she couldn't. Despite her resolve to keep him at arm's length, her emotions shot to the surface. "Damn straight!" she snapped and bolted to her feet.

Austin had seen Monica's offensive play enough times now to know when to push her and when to pull back. "I suppose now you're going to throw me off your property for coming to your rescue."

"My what?"

Knowing that sudden movements frightened ill-tempered animals, and believing Monica was as defensive as he'd ever seen her, Austin stood, holding his hands at his side in a surrendering posture. "Rescue."

"I didn't ask for your help. The way I recall it, you butted into my business…again!"

Smiling, he said, "It's no big deal. A simple 'thank you, Austin' would be appropriate."

She glared at him.

"I don't get it. Why is it so hard for you to accept the simplest act of kindness? It's just common courtesy to thank people."

"Is that why you keep making my problems your problems? You want me to thank you?"

"Suppose it is."

"You're lying. You want something from me and it's not just neighborliness," she fumed, feeling her cheeks flame. She wished she could remain calm, but there was something about Austin Sinclair that set her off. Half the time she wanted to pick a fight with him, and the other half she wanted... What was the matter with her that she couldn't stop thinking about him that way? He was nothing to her. Nothing. It had to remain like that. There was too much danger for her otherwise.

He swept her into his arms so quickly and clamped his mouth over hers with such expertise, Monica surrendered before she realized she'd been captured. Though it seemed impossible, his touch was more exhilarating than last time. The memory of the sweet taste of his lips against hers was nothing compared to the reality. The pressure of his mouth on hers was more demanding this time. There was an urgency to the way he parted her lips with his tongue as if he'd never kissed her before and never would again. Cradling her face in his hands, he slanted his mouth over hers, repeatedly demanding she meet his fire with her own. This time he wasn't interested in instructing her, pleading with her for favors or gently reminding her that he could elicit earthquakes under her feet.

This time he was taking.

His arms were stronger than she remembered as he crushed her breasts to his chest, where she could feel his rapidly pounding heart. Splaying his fingers, he stroked wide paths over her back, not missing the slightest curve of her shoulder blades, ribs or lower back. Pressing her closer to him, cupping her buttocks and grinding his erection into her pelvis, he made certain she knew precisely what was on his mind.

Breathlessly he kissed her again, his tongue foraging her teeth, the walls of her mouth and stroking her tongue. Like stone striking flint, she burst into internal flames until her need became greater than his.

She wanted to feel his touch on her breasts the way he'd done before. She wanted him to seek the most intimate parts of her body; to make her feel the way she'd felt in his arms only nights ago. She wanted this experience in its every facet, and to do that she needed a guide. She needed Austin.

Sinking to the soft, green grass together, Austin unbuttoned Monica's shirt and peeled it over her shoulders, exposing her breasts. "You're more beautiful than words can describe," he said, his voice low.

Unaccustomed to hearing flattery, Monica was surprised at the pleasure she felt hearing his words. "No one has ever said that to me," she replied honestly.

"Then they're idiots," he replied, and lowered his head noticing that just the touch of his breath against her skin caused her nipple to become erect. "You're even more sensual than you are beautiful."

His mouth swooped over the swell of her breast like a falcon on the hunt. Circling, then gliding in for the kill he captured her nipple between his teeth, then tugged gently, eliciting a cry of pleasure from deep inside her throat. "Austin..." She heard herself say his name like a prayer. "Please," she said sinking her fingers into his hair and pressing his lips deeper into her breast.

He stopped abruptly and moved his face over hers, though he continued to rub her nipple with his thumb. "What did you just say?"

"Please, Austin, I want..." Her eyes were swimming in tears—though she didn't feel sad—and she had a difficult time focusing. She wished she could see his expression. She wanted to know what he was thinking. Was he feeling what she was feeling? Was it possible she could elicit these same feelings in him?

"I've never heard you ask me for something."

Quickly he unzipped her jeans and slipped his hand over her abdomen. She shuddered. He slipped it lower still. She shivered in his arms, though she wasn't cold in the least. If anything she was hot, as if burning from the inside out.

His voice was so low and gutteral, sounding as if it were scraping over sandpaper, that she barely understood his question. "Tell me what you really want."

She remained silent as she placed her hand on his and pressed his hand lower. Then she pushed her jeans to her knees. Taking her lead, he leaned her back against the cool grass and finished taking off her clothes.

Kneeling at her feet, he boldly let his eyes take in every inch of her. Then he slid his hands from her neck to her breasts, paused for a moment as he filled them with her and then moved lower. He languorously spread her legs apart with his hands, watching the opening of her flower. He slipped his thumb on her protruding bud and pressed against it.

Monica's body jerked like a fish out of water as spasms of desire washed over her. He stroked her again with his thumb and she responded. Aware that with his every touch, an aching sensation inside her pulsed faster, she pressed her flesh against his thumb. Oddly, she was not self-conscious under his scrutiny. In fact, realizing his eyes were glazed with desire, she welcomed it. She wanted him to know everything about her.

Suddenly he stood and stripped off his clothes, then stretched out alongside her. His face hovered over hers, their lips nearly touching. "Look at me, Monica."

She opened her eyes, thinking she'd never seen anything more beautiful than the soft lights in Austin's eyes at that moment.

"I can stop right this minute. Walk away."

"Why?"

"I want you to know what you're doing."

"I do."

"Really," he smiled seductively, then blew lightly against her nipple. It hardened instantly. "You're on fire."

"I feel like I am."

"That's not rational. It's sexual. I want you so badly it hurts."

She touched his cheek. "Then make it stop hurting, Austin. Make it…"

His mouth devoured hers at the same instant his finger slipped inside her. The blade of his tongue dueled with hers while his fingers rubbed, stroked and taunted her sex. She felt as if every blood vessel in her body was pulsing to that rhythm Austin had awakened in her. Slaking her tongue against his, she forced a sensual groan from him.

He moved away from her for a moment to apply protection, then back again to push her legs apart with his knee. She felt his fingers leave her, to be replaced by his shaft. He stroked her bud with himself, making her feel as if she'd been struck by lightning. He was relentless in his torture, but he effectively molded her into a mass of sexual need and eagerness.

At the moment he entered her, she felt a delicious stretching as he filled her, but it was quickly followed by a sharp, stabbing pain. Had he not been kissing her, her scream would have brought the angels down from the mountaintops.

"It's over," he whispered as he slowly moved inside her. Pushing, pulling, sliding, stroking, her pain vanished in a watershed of desire.

Once again she felt herself rubbing against him, pushing herself onto him. Demanding with her gyrating hips that he enter her farther. Clamping her arms around his neck, she pressed her mouth against his.

He moaned.

She moaned.

He filled his hand with her breast and gently squeezed her

again, forcing another shooting pang from her breast to her loins. She raised her hips, hoping to bring him closer, deeper; knowing eternity was not long enough to remain fused together.

Her skin was on fire. Her insides were blazing. She felt trapped. She felt free.

She wanted to tell him things she never thought she'd say to a man.

Then he pushed himself so deeply inside her, her heart told her she'd been marked in an ancient, mythical way that bonded them through time and eternity.

His explosion catapulted her to another realm.

"Monica..." He breathed her name rather than spoke it. She'd never heard her name uttered with reverence, and the sound of it carried her to a place far beyond the pasture. She felt as if she were soaring through the cosmos; uninhibited and unafraid, knowing all the while that when she came back to earth she would be met with loving arms.

"Monica," Austin whispered gently as he nuzzled her neck. "Are you all right?"

She awoke from her flight among the stars to find herself lying beneath Austin. A sweet smile of gratitude lifted her lips. "Yes, Austin. I'm fine."

"You don't want to shoot me?" He tucked a strand of sweat-soaked blond hair behind her ear.

"No."

"Did I hurt you?"

"Yes, but only for a little while."

"It only hurts the first time."

"I know." Her face was filled with concern.

"What is it?"

"What happens if I start to feel like this again?" she asked.

"Then I'll have to take you again," he replied seductively.

"I was afraid you'd say that."

Ten

Of all the stupid ideas Austin had ever had, making love to
Monica in order to get her out of his system was just about
the dumbest.

Taking her once hadn't been nearly enough for either of
them. She had demanded a second time. He'd asked for a
third. It was long after nightfall when he drove her home in
his truck, her horse tied to the tailgate. Austin didn't think
he'd used the accelerator at all during the slow ride, but merely
coasted to her cabin. He'd kept his arm around Monica's
shoulder, and she'd pressed her face into his shoulder while
hugging his waist.

When they arrived at her cabin and she'd put Starshine up
for the night in the barn, Monica had shared the beauty of her
private lake with him.

They stood on the water's edge, solemnly undressing each
other. He was stunned at her beauty each time he saw her.
She looked like a moon goddess, he thought, and told her so.

No matter how many times he kissed her, entered her, it wasn't enough.

When it came to Monica, Austin was insatiable.

They dove and swam in the water, frolicking like children. He scooped her up in his arms and kissed her each time she came up out of the water. While she floated on her back, he licked her nipples. Turning her over on her tummy, he spread her legs apart and pulled her down on him. They kissed and caressed the night away and both were stunned when the rooster crowed.

"It can't be morning," he said, splashing water on his face.

"I'm afraid it is," she replied, swimming into his embrace.

He kissed her. "Have I overstayed my welcome?"

"I am a little tired." She yawned.

Pulling her out of the water and heading toward shore he suggested, "Then let's go inside and rest for a few hours."

"No!" she replied tersely. How could she tell him no man had entered her cabin since her grandfather had left? Not even Ted Martin had slept with her mother in the cabin. Monica had thought of the cabin as a sanctuary. If she were to allow Austin into the cabin, it was possible she might lose a piece of her soul. It was one thing to have given Austin her body. It was another to give him her heart.

"What's the matter?" he asked, still in a jovial mood, unaware of the tight clench of her jaw. "Are you afraid I'll criticize your housekeeping?"

"My what?"

"Housekeeping," he replied as he walked ashore and turned back to her.

Monica bent, snatched up her clothes and rolled them into a ball. "I think you should go."

Concern filled his voice. "Monica, what's wrong? Have I done something to upset you?"

"No."

"Then why do you want me to leave?"

"You have work to do. So do I."

"I understand that, but a few hours of sleep will do us both good." When he tried to pull her into his arms, she acquiesced woodenly. "There *is* something wrong."

Monica tried to step away from him, but Austin refused to release her. "You're making this difficult for me, Austin."

"What should be difficult about my wanting to hold you in my arms while I sleep?"

"I've never slept with anyone before."

"Did it occur to you that you might like it?"

"No."

Placing his forefinger under her chin, he lifted her face to his. "Maybe you'll like it more than lovemaking."

How was it possible to have kissed a man a hundred times in a single night only to discover it wasn't enough? What kind of spell was it that made her lose all concept of time and place when she was with Austin? The worst part was that she knew beyond equivocation that if he were to touch her breast again, she would want him all over again.

Just looking at him, she felt her sex begin pulsing. Was this how it was going to be with her? Perhaps she was doomed to be a victim of passion just like her mother.

She could resist his hypnotic eyes, but not his addictive kiss. He'd use them both to control her. She'd be no better off than Granny or Rose.

"That's impossible," she finally replied.

His warm smile was tentative as he asked, "Then it's not because of my lovemaking that you want me to leave?"

"No," she replied, peering into his eyes.

"Thank God," he said, and kissed her deeply.

Cold lake water slaked down her spine and puddled in the curve of her buttocks. Sliding her arms around his waist, she pressed her breasts against him, seeking his body's heat. He groaned and splayed his fingers over the soft rounded mounds of her hips. He grew hard again and slipped his fingers between her legs.

"Urrrgggggghhhhh. I'm beginning to see what you mean," he said. "If I don't go home, neither of us will get any rest. Nor will we get anything accomplished today."

Nodding, she said, "I think it would be best."

Slowly he pushed her away, though he continued kissing her. "I'm going. Really, I am," he chuckled.

"Then you might want your clothes," she smiled, handing him his jeans and shirt.

"Thanks." He started walking away, then turned around and looked at her. Holding the wad of her clothes to her side, she was unabashedly resplendent, he thought. He wanted to always remember her like this. Naked. Unafraid. Unadorned. Alone in nature.

He was suddenly struck by the thought that whether her pride would let her admit it or not, she needed him. Convincing her of this fact was not going to be easy.

"Monica?"

"Yes?"

"If I gave you a present, would you accept it?"

"What kind of present?" she asked.

"Something I believe you need. Something that would make me very happy if you would accept it. Please say you will."

"I don't need anything, Austin."

"You need this," he replied cheerfully stepping into his jeans and zipping them up. "Didn't your Granny tell you it's ungracious to refuse a gift?" He stuck his arms in his shirt.

"What is it, Austin?"

He got into the truck and leaned out the window. "You'll see." He waved and walked away.

Two days later Monica cocked the shotgun at the strange man approaching her cabin. "State your business or I'll

at her hips. He drew back again and aimed the [...]
went, her feet [...]

"Lower [...] the [...]

"I'm here to install the telephone."

"What telephone?"

"The one Mr. Sinclair ordered for you. The linemen have spent the last forty-eight hours stringing the wire from Mr. Sinclair's place up here. Didn't you hear the commotion out by the road yesterday when they put up the pole?"

"I did. I thought it was the road crew again. They come up every spring to regravel." She peered down the barrel at him.

Shrugging his shoulders, the man said, "I'll tell Mr. Sinclair you refused—"

"Never mind!" Monica shouted and uncocked the gun. She lowered it to her side.

"That's more like it. It's gonna take all damn day to get the rest of the wire strung over to the house."

"Put it in the barn," she ordered.

"Are you sure about that, ma'am? It's a long walk to the barn, and most folks aren't gonna let it ring that many times for you to pick up."

"That'd be fine. Nobody's gonna be calling me, anyway."

He scratched his head. Then nodding, he said, "That's *exactly* what Mr. Sinclair said you'd say."

"He did?"

"Yes, ma'am. It's right here on my work orders," he flipped the metal top back on his clipboard as he walked toward her.

"Let me see that," she said.

Showing her the work order, the man leaned down to pet Daisy. "Nice dog."

"Damn. He's persistent, isn't he?"

"Yes, ma'am," the phone man replied. "Running a line this far isn't cheap. May I suggest you might want to put the phone in the living room? Or the kitchen is always nice. That way you can talk while fixing supper or doing the laundry."

"The kitchen?"

"It's a practical place."

"The kitchen it is." Monica always thought of herself as being practical.

Austin used his portable phone when he punched out Monica's number for the first time. His workmen were cleaning up at the end of another long, though extremely productive, day. The kitchen cabinets were completely installed, as well as the last of the appliances, the brass faucets, beige porcelain sink and the quarter-round floor molding had been caulked and painted. Once Austin finished vacuuming the last of the sawdust, the kitchen would be gleaming.

The house was coming together, he thought. However, as Monica's phone rang for the fifteenth time, he thought *he* was coming unglued. "What is she doing?"

He hung up and dialed again. This time he let it ring twenty times.

The workmen drove away in their trucks as the sun disappeared behind the mountains; their radios blasting country-western tunes.

Austin flipped on the kitchen lights, still holding the portable phone to his ear. "Monica, I'm not giving up on this. If I have to stay on this thing all night long, I swear I'll—"

Concentrating on the phone call, he ignored the evening breeze fluttering through the house as the front door opened.

She glided across the living room and stood beneath the new antler chandelier that had been installed in the center of the dining area. "Swear you'll what, Austin?" she asked.

He jumped. "Holy—" He laughed. "Would you quit doing that?"

"Doing what?"

"Creeping up on me without warning," he said, putting the phone down and walking over to her.

"I don't see why I should. You don't have a lock on your

door. I do. You put a phone in my house without my permission. I think I should be able to come and go here as I please."

"Oh, you do, do you?" he pulled her into his arms.

"I do."

"You wore my favorite dress."

"It's all I have. How can it be your favorite?"

"It's the only one I've seen you wear. And if memory serves me correctly," he placed his hand on her breast. The nipple hardened instantly.

She gasped.

The top two buttons popped open.

He lowered his head. "Everything is just as I remembered," he said.

"Not everything," she replied pulling the side of her skirt up to her waist. "I left my underwear at home."

"Good thinking," he said hoisting her into his arms. He carried her into his temporary bedroom.

Through the undraped window, stars flickered above the mountaintops. The light from the living room seeped under the doorsill, like gloaming.

Monica was rapacious with desire. Two days away from Austin had proved only one thing to her. She'd made a terrible, irrevocable mistake when she'd let him kiss her the first time. Now she was worse off than her mother or grandmother had ever been. Maybe *they* had lived without a man, without lovemaking, but she couldn't.

Encircling her fingers around his manhood, Monica urged Austin to enter her, but he held back. Suddenly she was frightened.

"Did I do something wrong?" she asked.

"No, darling. I want us to go slowly tonight."

Feeling the delicious ache between her legs, Monica wasn't sure. "Why?"

"I'll show you," he replied with that low gutteral tone that sent waves of passion tumbling through her body.

Stringing hot, tiny kisses in ribbons over her breasts, down her stomach to her abdomen, Monica thought nothing he could do could be as agonizingly tantalizing. But she was wrong.

"Spread your legs, Monica. Open yourself as wide as you can. I want to kiss you."

Before she fully understood what he was saying, he pressed lightly on the insides of her thighs. Monica felt the light flutter of his tongue against her bud. Her cry was filled with shock and desire. She sank her fingers into his hair, hoping he would never stop.

Licking and stroking, biting and teasing, Austin coerced sounds from Monica's throat she hadn't known existed. His lips manipulated waves of deep, pulsing need inside her body while light, electriclike pricks bombarded her bud.

Her body gyrated in slow rhythmic circles, undulating beneath Austin's tongue, surrendering to his mastership.

This is heaven, she thought as she floated away from her body. This is what it's like to be an angel, looking down on the world, filled with nothing but love.

At that moment Monica was overflowing with love for the world. Discovering she was capable of forgiving the people who had hurt her was a revelation. She felt the bitterness inside her melt like winter snow when kissed by spring. In her mind's eye she could see the possibility of a world filled with peace and total harmony, and the joy of that place was more intoxicating than Austin's kiss. Her emotions swelled and ebbed in her heart, and she found she had more love to give than she'd ever imagined. She could see the chambers of her heart opening like wooden doors on rusty hinges, to reveal places of wonderment. She heard a baby's cry and then a small child's laugh. Whether the sound had once been her own or was the cry of the unborn, she didn't know, but in that instant she bonded with it, nurtured it.

Monica did not remember when Austin had entered her, because she realized they were one from the moment they'd kissed. To her, there was no division between foreplay and intercourse. Austin's lovemaking was a single rhapsodic symphony which they both created.

As if from a distance, she heard the sound of his voice. She wasn't certain why he would call her back from this plane in which she was one with all living and loving creatures and things. It seemed sacrilegious. For her soul to have traveled through the dimensions and made this discovery was wondrous yet vastly humbling.

When she opened her eyes to find herself cradled in Austin's arms, she burst into tears. Nothing she'd ever experienced, not the glory of the mountains, the power of winter storms, nor the gentle rebirth of spring, would move her soul this much again. She had discovered something so incredibly rare she deeply doubted her grandmother or mother even knew of its existence. Certainly they had never told of such things, never hinted of this awe-inspiring love.

Monica had discovered that mortals were divine.

"Why are you crying?" Austin asked, his voice riddled with concern.

"It was all so beautiful," she replied.

"I'm glad I made it that way for you."

"Didn't you see it?" she asked, wiping tears from her cheeks.

"See what?"

"I think it was heaven," she replied softly.

He touched her cheek. "That's the sweetest thing I've ever heard."

Though she saw sincerity in his eyes, she didn't find clarity as she'd hoped. He doesn't know what I'm saying! His experience wasn't the same at all!

She kissed the tips of his fingers. "How very sad," she replied despondently.

"Sad? I thought you said it was heaven."

"I meant that it wasn't the same for you," she said, and slid her leg out from under him.

With her movement Austin rolled to her side, though he kept her head cradled in his arm. The spell he'd been weaving had been broken. He could feel it dissipating like smoke.

Monica slipped out of the bed.

"Where are you going?"

She didn't want to look at him, now that she was filled with a plethora of fears. "Home."

"Please stay with me, Monica."

"I can't." She reached for her dress, which was lying in a puddle on the floor.

He bolted upright. "Why not? What's wrong with sleeping with me? What frightens you about being in the same bed with me all night?"

"I'm not afraid," she said defensively.

"Yes, you are. Look at you. Your hands are shaking so much you can barely button your dress. You let me make love to you, but you won't sleep with me. You're not making any sense."

"So, I must be crazy like everyone warned you."

"I didn't say that."

"It's true." *Now I've been to heaven, and you'll think I'm even more daft.*

She walked out of the room, but not before Austin bolted out of bed and stopped her.

"I'm not going to make you stay here," he said, holding her arm.

"Then what are you going to do?"

"Tell you that when you want to come back, I'll be here."

Monica felt her heart opening up all over again. A rush of love for him washed over her and encircled him. She didn't understand the things she was feeling, even seeing in her mind's eye. No one had prepared her for such intensity. One moment she wanted desperately to cling to Austin and never leave his side, yet the next, she heard her mother's warnings.

"Losing your heart to a man allows him to take over your mind. Once that happens, not even your thoughts and dreams are yours. He'll haunt you like a ghost. Awake or asleep, he'll make your life hell."

Having been taught nothing but fear all her life, Monica believed she had no choice but to escape. And she would never come back.

He watched her.

She left as she came, in the same rush of cool wind.

Eleven

Monica remained in a state of timelessness as she waded through the morass that muddled her life. Mending fences, moving her cattle to the low country, repairing the barn roof and scraping old paint from the west side of the cabin in preparation for a new coat exhausted Monica's body enough so that she craved Austin only every other minute.

She couldn't help thinking about Austin's work crew and the incredible amount of work they'd accomplished in a week, now a month. If only she had the money, she would replace the dilapidated fence her cattle had too easily trounced, then escaped through. Every head she lost was money out of her bank account. Necessary, too, was a new roof. A new truck. A new furnace. New plumbing. The list was endless.

For the first time Monica was beginning to see the folly of the life she'd led alone with her grandmother, trying to make her ranch profitable. Going over her accounts, she realized that despite the fact she'd made a great deal with Jake Simmons by selling the calves, she still wasn't breaking even.

"I'll bet Austin would know how I could bring in more money."

It was a good thing her pride kept her from asking for his help. Pride and common sense, she thought. She knew too well that if she went to him, she would want him again. And once again she faced her worst dilemma of all.

I'm in love with a man who doesn't love me in return, she thought.

It was as clear as the sunrise to Monica. She'd been to heaven, and Austin had not. Even further proof was the fact that if he loved her, he would have told her so. That much about men she *had* learned from her grandmother.

A woman in her situation was a fool if she didn't face reality and then deal with it. Unfortunately her energy levels were high. No amount of physical labor seemed to squash her thoughts about Austin or erase the memory of his lovemaking. Instead of sleeping at night, she swam in the lake. Eating held no particular pleasure other than to kill the hunger pangs in her stomach. But the most difficult part of all was ignoring the telephone when it rang.

Though the sound at first was strange as it echoed throughout the cabin, she grew used to the regularity of Austin's calls. Breakfast time, late afternoon when she came in from the pasture, then at supper time and once again just as she was about to fall asleep...or he was going to bed.

Her dreams never let her forget one moment she'd shared with Austin. Tossing and turning did her no good, so she left her dreams and opted to keep herself busy with work.

For months she'd been promising herself to go through Granny's old things in the barn loft. She knew the church in town would take old clothing and goods she didn't need. Looking at the mountain of junk piled in the barn loft, Monica mumbled to herself, "Where did it all come from?"

Pulling an old sheet off a mound of trunks and boxes, she coughed and batted at the dust clouds she'd raised.

She turned up the kerosene lantern in order to read Granny's handwriting on each of the boxes. Most of the boxes were bills and receipts, bundled with string and marked with the year. Monica was amazed to find grocery and lading bills dating back to the forties and thirties. She found a scrapbook her mother had made when she was a child. In it were yellowed photographs taken with Granny's old Kodak Brownie camera.

She was surprised to find her mother dressed in what looked like a cheerleader's uniform for the same high school Monica had attended. Numerous photographs depicted Rose in the center of a group of young boys and girls. Remembering her mother more as the sound of bitter words and angry epithets, Monica was drawn to the pretty blond girl sitting in a wood-paneled station wagon next to a boy who clearly had his arm around her shoulder.

Scrutinizing the photograph, Monica thought the boy looked familiar, but the colors had faded too much and dulled the clarity. She found other photos that told a story of her mother she'd never heard. Rose being crowned homecoming queen. Rose sitting at the soda fountain at Highstatler's Pharmacy wearing a pretty white dress and white wrist corsage. There were other girls around her, all smiling, all dressed much the same.

"Why, she's absolutely beautiful."

Monica found photographs of Rose standing next to the Statue of Liberty. Rose on a ship waving from the rail. Rose next to the Eiffel Tower. Rose next to a guard at Buckingham Palace.

At first Monica thought the photographs had lied to her somehow, but they told the truth. Her mother hadn't spent her life in seclusion on this mountain at all. Not only had she traveled in the United States, she'd been to Europe. Though the fact made little difference to her own experience with her mother, the knowledge sat dully on Monica's shoulders. Like a pesky fly, Monica couldn't get rid of the feeling she'd been duped.

Rose had obviously enjoyed a great deal of popularity in high school. There was no mistaking the adoration in the eyes of her friends. Somehow Granny had come up with the money to send Rose to Europe.

Flipping through the rest of the photographs, Monica found the backs marked with city names like Rome, Venice, Geneva, Vienna.

"All these years, Granny told me happiness was to be found on this mountain. That Montana was where the moon always shone the brightest. That seeing foreign places wasn't all it was cracked up to be. But for whose benefit was she saying it? Hers? Or mine? Maybe it was neither. Maybe it was for Rose."

Monica's mind swam in a whirlpool of unanswered questions. She couldn't dig through the photo albums and scrapbooks fast enough. More riddles came to light.

In one photo Rose was back in Montana, bearing the leather suitcase with dozens of stickers from foreign locales plastered on it, and the joy in her face had vanished. Monica regarded her mother's photograph and knew something dreadful had happened while she was in Europe.

Scrambling for answers, Monica discovered that the number of photographs of her mother dwindled to nothing. Her face became careworn, her hair long and her clothes faded and lifeless as the years passed. In only one photograph, marked 1976, bicentennial Fourth of July, did Rose's earlier beauty and exuberance shine.

"That's when she met Ted Martin."

Instantly Monica sensed the picture had been taken by her father.

Rose was sitting with her knees pulled to her chest on the edge of the lake. Her hair was curled and shining. But it was the anticipation, yet fulfillment, in her eyes Monica recognized because she'd seen the same look in her own reflection after Austin had made love to her.

Monica would have given anything to find a photograph of her father, to know what he looked like, if she resembled him in any way, but there were none. Whether Rose destroyed photographs of Ted Martin or simply hadn't taken them to begin with, Monica would never know.

Resentment built slowly in Monica's mind and heart as she continued her foray into her family's past. She was coming to realize how profound her mother's selfishness and self-pity had been. Not only had Rose sealed herself away from society after Ted Martin left, she had purposefully destroyed evidence, precious bits of truth about herself and Ted that might have quelled Monica's fears about the future.

Ironically, Monica realized the greatest culprit in this scheme was her beloved granny.

After all, it was Granny who retold Rose's story to Monica as she grew, purposefully leaving out huge chunks of vital information. Even more than facts about Ted Martin, Monica wanted to know about the high school boy in the faded photograph. Had Rose gone to Europe thinking that boy was in love with her, only to return to Silver Spur to find another girl had taken him away? Or was the scenario different? Had he discovered Rose's selfishness? Or Adelaide's obvious mastery at distorting truth?

Like an avalanche, fragments of comments she'd heard over the years rolled toward her, threatening her life as she knew it.

Even now, she could hear Doc's voice say, "Foster Skye was as rich as Croesus. He built this valley, but not with his bare hands."

"Your grandfather was a master builder," Adelaide had said, and Monica had taken her statement to mean that Foster had nailed every nail.

She realized that Foster had employed the townspeople,

given them jobs and a new focus...much like Austin Sinclair was doing now.

"Foster Skye was restless," Adelaide had said.

"Foster Skye was a man of vision," Vernon Highstatler had said once. "If it weren't for him and his money, most of us wouldn't have our livelihoods."

"Once he left here, he never looked back," Adelaide said. "He didn't want a family."

Voices from the past seemed to fill the old barn as never before. For the first time, Monica began puzzling their words into chronological order, matching them with the photographs.

A new story emerged, one she wasn't sure she wanted to hear, but one she was certain was the truth.

Adelaide had been young when she'd come to Montana with Foster. He was very wealthy and probably desired many of the conveniences his life back in San Francisco had afforded him. Silver Spur, according to Granny, had been a watering hole and nothing more. Foster, the man of vision, had seen the possibilities in this majestic land. Instead of holding on to his money, keeping it safe under the mattress, as Adelaide would have had him do, he, "the master builder," built more than the two-story cabin in which they lived.

It was Monica's guess that her grandfather put up the money to build Highstatler's Pharmacy. Though Vernon Highstatler was only a child at the time, his father benefited greatly. She reasoned there couldn't have been enough customers for the pharmacy to make a profit in the early 1930s. Perhaps Foster let the loan payments to himself ride for the time being. Perhaps the Highstatlers never paid the loan. Was it guilt that caused Bill Highstatler to tease her all these years? Did he carry his grandfather's financial burden?

There was the Methodist Church that also had the same Frank Lloyd Wright prairie design to it that reminded her of her cabin. Was it possible Foster had built it, as well? And the post office? The general store?

"Just how many people in town would owe my grandfather if he were alive?"

Was Foster's generosity too much for Adelaide to take? She, being the practical woman she was, never throwing even the rattiest towel away, was no doubt driven mad by his investments. Had she and her superciliousness driven Foster away?

Monica didn't have to ask herself why Adelaide didn't collect the old debts.

Pride.

Adelaide's pride kept her from relating to the townspeople. As long as she didn't ask them for their loan payments, they wouldn't castigate her for driving Foster away.

Yet it was obvious that Foster sent money to Adelaide. The money for Rose's beautiful high school wardrobe and her European trip didn't come from cattle sales. Especially not back then.

There was no question in Monica's mind, that though Foster didn't physically return, his money did.

Monica looked at her mother's photographs with closer scrutiny. Was it possible Rose was liked for her father's money? Or at the very least, she must have felt she was.

Suddenly Monica knew the identity of the boy in the wood-paneled station wagon...Vernon Highstatler. Had Vernon truly been in love with her mother? Or was he courting her because his father pushed him to it? Whichever the reason, it all ended when Rose returned from Europe. It would be interesting to know if that summer Vernon had married Bill's mother. However, there was no question that when Vernon married, Rose was devastated. Monica believed that his rejection had caused Rose to become even more bitter toward her father.

Summing up her findings, Monica came to the conclusion that the one constant in all these machinations was Adelaide.

The paradigms that had framed Monica's life, her every thought, goal and belief had come from Adelaide. She'd never once questioned her grandmother's word. Adelaide had been her only source of nurturing, caring. She'd been the only person to love her.

Until now. Until Austin.

The truth stung Monica's eyes as she dropped the photographs from her hands. Adelaide had betrayed her by keeping the truth from her. She'd planted twisted thoughts in her head she was afraid were impossible to eradicate.

She felt as if she were suffocating. Dying.

"I have to get out of here...breathe—" She stumbled backward over one of the boxes and knocked the kerosene lantern off its perch. It crashed. Glass flew everywhere. And from the metal hull, a serpent of fire slithered across the loft and ignited the mountain of very old, very dry keepsakes.

Austin adjusted the specially ground lens of the telescope he'd had shipped from Chicago. He'd splurged on the burled wood, copper and brass beauty when he'd banked his first million. Since he'd worn out his welcome at the Adler Planetarium before his tenth birthday, he surmised that on an adult level, stargazing should be a private affair.

Focusing on Monica's cabin, he tightened the set screws. "I guess now I'm a bona fide Peeping Tom," he said to himself squinting through the lens.

The cabin was illuminated on the first floor, but he saw no signs of movement. "She must be reading in bed."

Then he saw a lace curtain move in what he guessed was the living room. There was no one at the window. Lowering the telescope, he caught sight of a small dark figure who brushed the curtains back, disappeared and then returned again to pull back the curtain.

"Daisy."

There was something frantic about the dog's behavior. He realized Daisy was barking. Not a little but a lot. Had he been closer, her barking would have been enough to wake the dead.

"Where the hell are you, Monica?"

Suddenly, he realized the outside of the cabin was bathed in a bright light...too much light for the middle of the night.

Moving the telescope along the light's path, he gasped. "God Almighty!"

Flames shot out the roof of the barn, and smoke billowed out of the loft opening. A figure dangled on a rope just outside the second-story loft hatch.

"Monica!"

Austin raced to the kitchen, grabbed the Tahoe keys and snatched his muddy runners, which were just outside the front door. Before jumping into the Tahoe, he riffled through what seemed like a ton of equipment he'd bought.

"It's in here somewhere." Feeling the long plastic tubing, he clutched the sump pump and then scooped up an extralong utility extension cord still in the box.

"If ever I've asked You for a favor, do it now," he prayed. "Don't let anything happen to her."

Monica could hear Starshine whinnying in the stall below. The fire spit sparks around her bare feet, trapping her. Knowing that if she could get to the loft door, she could swing down on the bale lifter and free Starshine, she shouted to the horse, "I'm coming!"

She jumped over the fast-burning debris, beating a finger of fire as it raced behind her. She unlocked the door and instantly realized that after the last time she used the rope and pulley she'd swung it off to the side. She couldn't reach the rope from the platform where she was standing. She only had one choice; jump for the rope.

Daisy's frantic barking caught her attention just as she was about to leap. "It's okay, girl!" she shouted, but Daisy couldn't hear her.

Flames shot up around her, framing her in dangerous light.

She screamed as she leaned out as far as she could and pushed herself off the edge of the loft.

She missed the rope.

At least her fingers had, but her legs had instinctively entwined themselves around the familiar childhood shimmy. It took her a moment to realize she was upside down. She righted herself and ratcheted downward, hitting the ground with a thud. Not losing a second she burst back into the barn without a single thought about herself.

"I'm coming, Starshine!"

The horse banged at the stall door with raised forelegs.

Monica knew her screams would only frighten the horse more. She tried to be calm, but she was riddled with panic.

"Stay back! I'll get the door."

Starshine's dark eyes reflected the mounting, searing flames in the loft. Illuminated clumps of hay fell and ignited a bale on the lower level.

Austin had never driven so fast in his life. By the time he reached Monica's, the barn roof and upper-story walls were engulfed in flames. Daisy was still barking at the cabin window, but Monica was nowhere in sight.

"Monica!" he called.

Nothing.

The sound of horse hooves thundered over the crackling inferno.

"She's gone back inside!"

He grabbed his equipment and rushed toward the barn.

Clinging to Starshine's mane, Monica rode her horse through a wall of flame, her blond hair flying dangerously close to the fire.

Austin's heart stopped as he waited for her to clear the flames. From his vantage point he could see the second story caving in behind her. At the same moment, what was left of the roof crumbled, the framework shrinking as fast as a match stem. The sound of crashing lumber, screaming whorls of heat and fire and Starshine's hoofbeats rang terror through Austin.

"Monica!" he yelled and rushed alongside her as she rode the horse to safety across the clearing.

"Austin!" she cried pulling Starshine to halt and sliding off.

"You're on fire!"

He pushed her to the ground and rolled her over in the dirt. Using his jacket he smothered her hair.

"Oh, my God! Oh, my God!" She heard her screams, but she didn't feel any pain.

But she smelled searing flesh.

Not Starshine's. Mine.

"Help me!" she cried and submitted to him.

He ripped the smoldering cloth from her back, tossing it toward the inferno. With his hands he staunched the last of the fire in her hair.

"Monica! Oh, my God, I almost lost you!" He pulled her to the safety of his arms.

She folded into him.

Kissing her quickly he surveyed her face. She was in shock but there were no burns or cuts he could see.

She grabbed his hands as he touched her cheek. "You're trembling."

"You frightened the hell out of me. Are you okay?"

"Okay?" She almost didn't understand the question.

"God, your arms are peppered with burns."

"They are? I don't feel anything."

Shock. She's in shock.

"Here, put on my shirt. You've got to stay warm."

"You're crazy. I'm burning up from the heat." *Or am I cold? I can't tell.*

Austin covered her naked skin with his shirt, then his jacket. "My God, you were nearly killed!"

"But I wasn't—" she turned back toward the fire. "The

barn...all my equipment is in there!'' She started to run back toward it.

"Don't be foolish!'' Austin yelled. ''It's too late for that stuff. We have to save what's out here...and the cabin!''

"The cabin.'' She looked toward the house and saw Daisy.

"Come on,'' he ordered and grabbed his equipment. ''Is there an electric outlet at the back of the house?''

"No, but there's one in the bathroom.''

"Good. Take this cord and plug it in. I'll put this in the lake.''

"What is this thing?''

"A fire extinguisher.''

Austin tossed the sump pump into the lake and unrolled the eighty-foot-long plastic tubing through which he could transmit enough water to wet down at least some of the surrounding area. ''Back your truck away from the fire.''

Monica sprinted to the kitchen, got her keys and the frantic Daisy and moved the truck out of harm's way.

Austin valiantly fought the fire, but the inferno had fueled itself to monstrous proportions. He wetted down the side of the cabin closest to the barn to keep the fire from spreading. He drenched the front porch, as well.

The truth of the matter was there was little he could do except hold Monica while they watched the barn burn to the ground.

By sunrise, it seemed to Monica that half of Silver Spur was camped on her property. Some, like Doc and Myrna, had come to help, and others came out of curiosity.

Austin dealt with the townspeople, answering their ridiculous, intrusive questions, and finally persuaded them to leave. To those who sincerely offered their help, Austin promised they would form a cleanup crew to sift through the debris once the cinders had cooled.

Doc inspected Monica's burns and found that except for a

few bad burns on her back, most would heal without scars. He applied burn ointment to her arms and neck and dressed the more-serious wounds on her back.

"Will I be okay?"

"Right as rain in a few weeks. We'll have to watch these two patches on your back to make certain there's no staph infection. I want to see you every day for a week, young lady."

"Doc, I can't—"

"Will you give it up, Monica?" Austin interrupted. "I'll take you to town myself."

"It's not that," she said turning back to Doc. "I can't pay you all at once."

"We'll work something out," he said, patting her knee affectionately. "You're a very lucky lady you didn't burn your beautiful face."

"But half my hair's gone," she said.

Doc chuckled. "Now's a good a time to try the beauty shop in town."

"I haven't got money for things like that. Certainly not now."

Austin smiled. "I think we can scrape up the twenty bucks," he said.

"Fourteen. Includes blow-dry," Myrna said handing Doc clean gauze.

"A real bargain," Austin grinned.

Monica remained silent. She wasn't used to effusiveness and charity. She felt uncomfortable.

Austin watched the expression on Monica's face that night turn from shock to confusion to distrust. Something more than just the fire had happened to Monica that night. What had she been doing in the barn in the first place? Why had she gone there so late? And what could have made her so careless as to knock over a lantern she'd used since she was a child? None of it made any sense, but he wasn't leaving until his questions were answered.

Doc stood. "Get some rest, and I'll see you tomorrow."

Monica's eyes darted warily toward the smoldering barn. "I'll try."

Doc looked to Austin. "She needs to sleep. If she gets stubborn about it, get her drunk."

Austin chuckled. "I'll do my best," he said as he and Monica walked to the front porch with Doc and Myrna.

Doc and Myrna drove away thinking they were the last to leave.

Twelve

"**W**hat happened tonight?" Austin asked Monica.

"My barn burned!" She looked at him as if he were a fool.

"But how? And I don't mean you accidently knocked over the lantern."

"I'm telling the truth."

"Yes, but not all of it."

"There's nothing else to tell," she replied flatly, and sat in the straight-back chair opposite her grandmother's rocker. Funny. It looked different to her now.

Seat of betrayal.

She doubted she'd ever sit in it again. She should have tossed it into the fire.

"I don't like the damning look in your eyes," Austin said. "You want to talk about it?"

"No."

"Ah! So, there is something going on I don't know about."

Bolting to her feet, her anger spewed like lava. "You? What have you got to do with anything that happens to me?"

He tried to put his arms on her shoulders, but she shrugged him off. "I was trying to help is all," he retorted.

"I don't want your help."

"Is that so?"

"Okay. I don't need your help."

"Need I remind you that a few hours ago I saved your life?"

"I saved my own damn life! I got Starshine and myself out of that fire without you or anyone else." With every word she felt colder. She hugged herself, but it did no good. "All those people here…they don't give a damn about me! Ghouls. All they wanted was to watch the witch burn."

"Monica," he said softly.

"You're right, Austin, there was something going on tonight. Call it revelation. Call it apocalypse. It doesn't matter. They're the same."

"Baby…" He tried to reach for her, but she stepped away from him. He didn't like the way her eyes had glassed over.

A low chuckle mounted to laughter. Wild laughter. "You know what it was, Austin? It was hell's fire tonight. It came and washed away the sins."

"Whose sins?"

"Mine."

"But you haven't done anything wrong."

Her eyes were frantic as she looked out the large living room window. "My grandmother's sins. My mother's. They were the ones who started the fire. Not me. They just used me. All my life…they just used me. Maybe they thought I'd die in the fire. Maybe that's what they had intended to happen. But I fooled them both. I lived."

Austin didn't know how to treat hysteria. CPR was one thing. This was another. He had to trust his instincts. And he had to remain calm. No matter what.

"Monica, sweetheart. Let's not talk about them now."

"But you asked me to!"

"I did? When?"

"They are the 'something' that happened."

Gently he put his hands on her shoulders. This time she accepted him. He turned her to face him. "Slow down and tell me exactly what you were doing in the barn."

"Thinking. Looking at old photographs. That's all," she replied in a voice one octave too high.

Austin was frightened for her. He wished to hell he'd insisted Doc give her a sedative. But Doc didn't believe in drugs. He believed in whiskey...*and the truth.*

"Monica, you found something in the photographs you didn't know about before. Is that it?"

She nodded woodenly.

"What?"

"Lies. All lies." She heaved the words out of her chest with a sigh. "Granny lied to me. All my life she told me things that aren't true."

"Tell me about them," he said.

"I can't," she replied, her eyes becoming distant and unfocused.

"Yes, you can. You have to. It's very important to me."

She didn't want to look at Austin, but he was making her do it.

"It hurts." The betrayal stabbed deep inside her. In her heart and in her gut.

"Do it!"

"Okay!" She licked her lips. Dry. I feel burned and dried up. Ashes to ashes.

"What did Granny lie to you about?" Austin cradled her face in his hands, his thumb gently tracing her jawline. "She told you never to trust a man, didn't she, Monica?"

"Yes."

"She said the same thing to your mother, didn't she?"

"Yes."

"Do you think your grandmother was the reason your father left your mother?"

"Yes." Tears filled her eyes.

"She's the reason you never got to know your father."

"Yes."

"And you blame your grandmother?"

"Yes. She lied to my mother. She told my mother things that weren't true about my grandfather. She told the same things to me. She made the people hate her. Hate my mother. Hate me…"

"Calm down, sweetheart, and tell me how."

She took a deep breath and continued.

"Oh, Austin. I don't know if I'll ever really know for sure. I have suppositions and questions running around in my head. I think my grandfather and the townspeople got along very well. They liked him. He didn't just build this cabin, but Highstatler's Pharmacy, the City Hall, church and more. It was his money they borrowed. He was proud of his work, but Granny resented his time away from her. She wanted to keep him all to herself. She did the same thing with my mother.

"When Mother fell in love with Vernon Highstatler, Granny sent Mother off to Europe. Somehow she'd gotten the money out of my grandfather. I found letters of their correspondence to each other over the years. When Mother came back, Vernon was either engaged or already married. Then when Mother found love again with my father, Granny ran him off, too. She told me all my life that everything I needed was on this mountain. That I'd only find heartbreak and pain in the outside world."

"And that any man who loved you was not to be trusted."

"Yes. That's why I never went out with any of the boys in high school. I always raced back here. Back to Granny. I thought she loved me."

She burst into sobs.

Austin sighed. "She loved herself more."

Folding her into his arms, Austin held her gingerly against his chest, remembering the burns on her back. "Cry all you want, baby. Cry till you can't cry anymore."

Austin held Monica for what seemed an eternity, easing his weight back and forth in a rocking motion. For a moment he thought he'd lost her while her mind tried to escape her pain. But he had faith in her inner strength.

Carefully lifting her in his arms he carried her into the bedroom on the first floor. He laid her on the bed and stretched out next to her, never letting her out of his arms.

Finally she managed to say, "You don't have to stay. I'll be all right."

"I want to stay."

"I don't feel like making love, Austin."

"Neither do I," he replied, and pulled her closer. "I just want to hold you, if you'll let me."

"It feels safe here," she replied softly, and fitted her head in the crook of his neck.

"You are safe with me." *But am I safe with you?*

The next morning Austin inspected the cabin for photographs of Adelaide. He found two in the living room, one in an upstairs bedroom and one in the kitchen. He placed them in a group on the kitchen table and studied them as he paced back and forth with a mug of hot coffee to help him piece together Monica's story.

After what Monica had been through, it was a wonder she wasn't crazy.

The old woman had done a number on her granddaughter, all right. Austin didn't know much about psychology but he did know that his breezy affair with Monica had come to a crashing halt.

"If that's what it had ever been in the first place." He groaned, realizing he was more deeply involved with Monica's well-being than he'd thought.

Austin had come to this mountain as a cure for his career burnout and to mend what he thought was his broken heart. Now he realized his pain didn't come close to the kind of betrayal Monica was experiencing. Compared to hers, his past was a cakewalk.

If Adelaide were still alive, Austin would have wanted to throttle the old bat for what she'd done to both Rose and Monica.

"But she's dead, Austin, and there's nothing you can do about that." He scratched his head.

Since when have I become Monica's savior? he asked himself. Since the day I laid eyes on her.

"What are you doing?" Monica asked from the doorway.

Austin jumped. "I didn't see you there."

"I know. What are you doing here?"

"Here? You asked me to stay last night."

Shaking her head, she replied wearily, "I don't think so."

"I had a feeling you wouldn't remember it that way."

She walked over to the stove and removed the speckled cast-iron coffeepot. She took a cup off the dish drainer. "Thanks for making the coffee."

"You're welcome."

Casting him a sidelong glance, she pointed to the table. "You do that?"

"Yes."

"Why?"

"I wanted to get to know her. Maybe help you figure out her motivations about what she did to you."

She gave a slight nod. "I thought so." Taking a deep breath, she sat in a chair. "Austin, I know I said a lot of crazy things last night. It was the shock of the fire."

"Don't lie to me now, Monica. I was there, remember? I held you all night while you cried."

"Oh, God." She lowered her eyes.

"Look, there's nothing to be embarrassed about. You went

through hell last night. But you survived. In more ways than one. I don't know that I would have fared as well as you."

"I don't feel so well."

"I wouldn't think so." He crouched on his knees next to her. Tentatively he placed his hand over hers.

She didn't shake him off.

It was a good sign.

"Monica, I want to help you through this."

"This? What is this, Austin? Huh? Everything I've believed has been shot to hell. It's like I don't know who I am anymore. Or what I'm doing here. Or even what I want. Everything is such a mess."

"I know who you are."

"Yeah? And who is that?"

"A beautiful soul who has taken a beating all her life, thinking she's up against the entire world...by herself. She's strong. And good. And giving."

"And she's a fool."

"I don't see that at all."

"Then look harder. Monica Skye was so damn dumb she never once thought for herself. She lived out her grandmother's dreams for her. She's mindless."

"Look, what do you want me to do, Monica? I'll do anything you say."

Her eyes glittered like hard glass when she peered at him.

Austin felt the blood drain from his face. He'd never seen her like this, and he didn't like it.

"I want to find out who I am, Austin."

"That's good."

"I think so, too."

"Then what's the problem?"

She withdrew her hand from beneath his. "I don't want you around while I do it."

He swallowed hard. He hadn't bargained for this turn of events. "I don't think that's a good idea."

"Well, it's my life and I do," she replied adamantly.

He matched her hard gaze with one more determined. "Okay. My bet is you're wrong. But you have to find that out for yourself, as well. I'll leave you alone. For as long as you want."

"Fine."

He pointed to the telephone. "But if you change your mind, all you have to do is pick up that phone. Promise me you'll do it."

"And if I don't?"

"I'm not leaving."

"Okay. I promise. But I won't change my mind."

"Are you always this stubborn?"

"Yes."

Austin found he couldn't move from his spot. Something was making him stay. What the hell was the matter with him? He should walk out of here. Leave her to her thoughts. It was good she was smart enough to know she needed time alone. But damn it. He wanted her to want his help. But why? He'd never been the Good Samaritan type before. He was a mover and shaker. He was a guy who used acquaintances to build his roster, beef up his portfolio. Why should he care if this girl needed him?

There was only one answer. He was losing it worse than she was.

"I'm leaving," he said.

"Then do it," she ordered, staring off into the distance.

Finally he turned and left the cabin.

She jerked when she heard the door slam.

I was right, she thought. He doesn't love me. He had the perfect opportunity to say he did. He's just being kind to me. Neighborly. Just like the Harrisons used to be. I shouldn't take it for any more than that.

Monica looked down at her hands.

Amazing.

She'd gripped the cup so tightly she'd broken off the handle.

Monica needed answers. She drove the wobbling truck to town to see Doc.

Doc changed the dressings on her back, applying antibacterial and antifungal ointment to her burn. "I'm going to tell you now, Monica, that your burns here are pretty bad. You're going to have scars."

"I don't care about that," she lied.

"And I also know you have to be experiencing a great deal of pain, just to move. Seldom do I ever give pain medication, but I'm making an exception in your case."

"I don't need anything, Doc."

"Yes, you do. You're just too proud to ask for it."

"Proud?"

"A Skye trait to be sure," he said going to the closed cupboard and taking out a box of sample pills. "Take these home. Take one every six hours. No more than four a day. Last night you were in shock, which dulls pain. By now the healing process has set in. It's rough."

"I'll take them," she said, looking at the printing on the box but not reading the words.

He studied her for a long moment. "What is it, Monica?"

"You liked Granny, didn't you?"

"Of course. Admired her...faults and all."

"Faults?"

Doc chuckled. "Well, you know them as well as anyone, I suppose."

"I'm not sure that I do. Tell me, what did you think was her biggest fault?"

He scrutinized her. "Where's this coming from, Monica?"

She paused for a long moment. "When I was in the barn last night I found a bunch of old photographs. I saw things...odd things. Things that didn't match up with the stories Granny had told me about herself. And my mother."

Doc stiffened. "Your mother?"

"What do you know, Doc?"

"I think it best you tell me what *you think* you've discovered. Then I'll edit as you go along."

Monica related her story and the conclusion she'd drawn about Rose being in love with Vernon Highstatler. "Is that true or not?"

"It's true."

"Then why didn't anyone tell me? Why didn't *you* tell me?"

"What good would it do? What change would it make in your life?"

"I might have at least understood why the Highstatlers look at me like I have the plague whenever I walk into the pharmacy."

"They don't."

"They do. And that's another thing. Do you know if my grandfather loaned them the money to build?"

"Sure did."

"Why didn't I know that?"

"I never realized you didn't. Again, I ask, what difference would it make?"

"I...I..."

"What?"

"I don't know."

"Think about it."

"That's exactly what I've been doing." She sighed.

"Don't look so forlorn. No one, including your grandmother, was trying to do you a disservice. Maybe Adelaide had her reasons for not going into detail about some things, but so what? I'll be the first to admit, she was self-centered and autocratic, but so what? She loved you. Cared for you. Took care of you. That's more than some folks do for their kids."

"She fixed it up so my mother wouldn't marry Vernon Highstatler."

He scratched his chin whiskers. "I told her that was a mistake. She wouldn't listen. She was stubborn like you. And too proud."

"There's that word again."

"Pride?"

"Yeah. Somebody else told me I've got too much pride."

Doc smiled. "I wonder who that could be? Hmm?"

Monica straightened her blouse over her shoulders. "I'd better be going. I've got some errands."

"Sure." He eased himself off the rolling stool.

"Thanks, Doc."

"I want to see you tomorrow," he reminded her.

She agreed and left.

Clutching a twenty-dollar bill in her hand, Monica went to the beauty shop.

Pride.

Austin had offered to pay for her much-needed haircut, but she'd refused. She would pay her own way.

"May I help?" the peroxided blond woman behind the counter glanced at Monica and gasped. "What the hell you been using on your hair, honey? It's burned to a crisp!"

"It was an accident."

The woman's eyes crinkled. "Why, you must be Monica." She stuck her hand toward Monica. "Pleased to meet you. I'm Grace. I heard all about you."

Monica instantly bristled and prepared to defend herself as she'd always done. "What did you hear?"

"About that awful fire last night. Saints alive! We could see the flames shootin' to the moon from Main Street. What a sight! Sure am glad nothin' happened to you, honey."

Monica couldn't believe her ears. This woman sounded truly concerned about her. "You are?"

"Of course. Now you just come on over here and let me look at that hair of yours."

Grace pushed her down into a chair that reminded her of the chairs in the barbershop next door. A pale pink cape whisked through the air to surround Monica's neck and shoulders like a cloud.

"That's a bad burn on your neck, honey. I won't tie the cape, just clip it so's not to hurt you."

"You're very kind," Monica replied.

"Just bein' myself," Grace chirruped. "Now what did you have in mind?"

"I...I don't know."

"Well, how do you see yourself?"

See myself? she wondered. How should I know? I feel as if I was just born last night.

"Most of this will have to come off," Grace said.

"I don't know much about hairstyles. I've just let it grow. Wash it. That's about all."

"Incredible," she said gliding her fingers through hunks of her hair. Grace looked at Monica's reflection in the mirror. "With your eyes and high cheekbones, I'd like to suggest angling the hair around your neck, feathering it toward your face, with a slight bang effect to the right side, like this," she said holding the hair in place.

"Sure. I guess."

"There's not a whole lot I can do, since you've lost large chunks of hair from the back. I'll cut it so it'll just brush your shoulders and will cover the burns on your neck."

Grace peered at Monica's reflection. "It'll be lovely. Trust me."

"Okay." Monica swallowed hard.

The entire process from start to finish took half an hour. When Monica held up a hand mirror so that she could see the back of her hair, she couldn't help her approving smile. "It's beautiful."

"You're beautiful, honey. All I did was use your hair to bring out your features to their very best."

"I can't believe it."

"If you don't mind my saying, you've been hiding your looks under a basket. Would you mind if I made another suggestion?"

"What?"

Grace scrambled across the room and returned with a plastic tray filled with cosmetics. "Let me do your makeup?"

"No, thanks." Monica waved her hand in front of her face. "I don't want to look like a hussy."

Grace burst into laughter. "Who said you would?"

Granny.

Monica studied her reflection. How did she know what she would look like with makeup if she'd never tried it before? Already she liked her new haircut more than the way she'd worn it all her life. Grace had proven she could be trusted.

She smiled at Grace. "Okay, but not too much."

Grace knit her brows. "I want you to see how beautiful you really are. I'm not into clowns."

Monica liked the fact that Grace showed her how to roll the mascara onto her lashes and line her eyes with the tiniest smudge of brown kohl.

"They're twice as blue."

"Your skin is nearly perfect, but you should use sunblock if you're going to be outdoors all the time. When you're my age, you'll thank me. A little pale blush and just a hint of lip gloss is all I'd suggest you use. Unless it was a special occasion."

"Special?"

"Yeah, like—" she glanced outside at the banners being strung across Main Street announcing the Summer Festival dance and dinner the next weekend "—like if your fella was taking you to the festival."

"I've never been to the festival. I guess I won't be needing anything."

"You mean he saved your life, but he won't take you to the dance?"

"Who?"

"Your fella. Mr. Sinclair."

"Austin and I are just neighbors," she said, feeling a blush begin at her toes and rise up her back.

"That's not the way I heard it." Grace slapped her hand over her mouth. "Oooomph!"

"Really? What have you heard, Grace?" Monica skewered Grace's eyes.

Flustered, Grace's effort at retreat were futile. "I shouldn't have said anything. I'm sorry."

"I'm not. Tell me exactly how you heard it, Grace."

"Exactly?"

Monica nodded. "Don't worry. I won't tell anyone where I heard it. And if you tell me the truth, I'll return the favor by always coming to you for my haircuts."

Grace took a deep breath. "I heard you and Austin were more than neighbors. Lovers, actually. That he bought the largest box of condoms Highstatler's carries."

Austin had said they were being safe so she wouldn't get pregnant.... "Well, I can't govern how Mr. Sinclair spends his money, nor how others interpret his actions. Nor would I speculate on those purchases. It's none of my business, is it, Grace?"

"No."

"Why would anyone conclude I was the one Austin was—"

"Because he helped you with Jake Simmons...Trace said."

"Trace?"

Graced nodded solemnly.

Monica's lips thinned. "Tell me the rest."

"She said she watched you."

"Watched us?" Monica gasped. "Where? When?"

"Last night. At your cabin. She said Austin stayed all night."

"I supposed she was in my bedroom, huh?"

"Well, no…"

"She should have been. Because if she had been she would have known that nothing happened. He held me all night because I was hysterical. Didn't make any sense I was crying so much. But she didn't bother to learn the truth, did she?"

Monica bolted out of the chair, whipping the cape from her neck, not feeling the sting of the neckband against her burns. "What is it about the truth that nobody wants to see?"

"I dunno."

Reaching into her jeans pocket, Monica pulled out the twenty-dollar bill. "Will this be enough?"

"More than enough. I'll get your change."

Monica breathed deeply to calm herself. Gently she closed her hand around Grace's fingers. "No. You keep it. You've given me more than I can ever pay."

"I didn't do much," Grace replied.

"Yes, you did, Grace. And you know what? I think you're a real friend for being straight with me."

"I like you, Monica."

For a moment she was stunned. "I like you, too."

It was more than curiosity that spurred Monica toward the pharmacy—the gossips' gathering place. She couldn't help inspecting the architecture, wondering if it looked different to her now that she knew the truth of how it had come into being.

It looked the same.

As she reached for the glass door it opened.

Trace stepped into the sun. "Monica? Is that you?"

"Yes."

"I hardly recognized you. What did you do to yourself?"

"Ran through fire. You ever do that, Trace?"

"No." Her back stiffened. She took a step backward.

Monica advanced on her. Her eyes slid across Trace's face like hot lasers. "Get ready. Your turn's coming."

Forcing a smile, Trace's bottom lip quivered nervously. "What's the matter with you, Monica? You're talkin' crazy again."

"No I'm not. You're the one who's been talking too much."

"Huh?"

"Word is you've been saying Austin Sinclair and I are lovers. That you were peeking in my windows watching him make love to me last night."

"I never—"

"Damn straight you never did. 'Cuz that's not what happened at all. Somehow I think you know that. Know what I think?"

Trace kept taking one halting step backward after another. "What's that?"

"I think this is a case of the pot calling the kettle black."

"I don't get it."

"Maybe you've been shacking up with Austin and don't want anyone to know."

"That's ridiculous."

"I don't think so. I think you're spreading rumors about me so no one knows what you've been doing. If you're not sleeping with Austin, who is it?"

"Nobody."

Monica watched Trace flinch with each new question. She'd hit the target. Now she went for the kill. "Jake Simmons's wife would be real upset if she knew the truth. So upset, she'd make sure Jake fired you. Then what would you do?"

"You wouldn't dare!"

"Don't push me, Trace. You stay off my back, and I'll stay off yours. Do you understand me?"

"Yeah."

"Fine. Then I'll be seeing you around."

Monica flipped a wave and left Trace standing on the street corner looking as if she'd just raced through hell.

And she had.

That I hear. I'll be seeing you around.

Monica hung up again and felt three numbers on the rotary before realizing it was a just a dial (flowing bell)
and she had

Thirteen

—

It took three days for Austin to break his promise. He counted five rings before Monica picked up the telephone.

"I know I'm not supposed to be calling you," he said anxiously, "but I had to know if you're all right."

"I'm fine."

Fine. She's fine. Hell. "Do you need anything?"

"No."

A hand to hold? My company? "I saw Doc in town. He said you were healing well."

"It hurts, but I'm managing."

Why is this so hard for me? "Listen, Monica. I was thinking that maybe...well, you'd like to come for dinner tonight."

"I ate an hour ago."

It's that late? "I should have called earlier."

"It must have slipped your mind."

"Slipped my mind?" I just want to be with you. I want to see you, touch you, be in your presence. I want to know you think about me. Just a little.

"The invitation to dinner. You probably had other things on your mind."

No joke, he thought. Forget wanting...needing to be with you. God, do you have any idea how good it is to hear the sound of your voice? Do you know I'm smiling now? I haven't smiled in days. Maybe forever. "My house is almost wrapped up, they tell me."

"That's nice."

"Yeah, the master bedroom is really looking great. I can't wait for you to see it."

Silence.

"I meant—" Damn it.

"I know what you meant."

"No, you didn't." How could you? I'm only beginning to understand it myself.

"Austin, I have to go."

"No! Please don't hang up." It's too soon. I want you to stay on this phone and talk to me all night. "How about dinner tomorrow?"

"I can't."

"Can't? Or don't want to?" He held his breath.

"Don't want to."

"I was afraid of that." Just when I'm realizing how much you mean to me, you're realizing you never really wanted me in your life in the first place.

"Please don't sound like that, Austin."

"Like what?"

"Like I've died or something."

No, you're not dead. But something's died. He changed tactics. "Tell me the truth. How is it going for you? Are you discovering yourself like you thought you would?"

"I think so."

"But you're not sure?"

"I'm not sure."

"What are you not sure about?" He clung to fine threads of hope.

"That maybe I wasn't so lost after all."

"Really?"

"Austin, I've realized I have you to thank for helping me."

"It was nothing. I've saved damsels before," he teased.

"I didn't mean about the fire. Or the sale with Jake. I meant that knowing you has been one of the best experiences of my life."

She's speaking in the past tense. Am I ever going to see her again? "I'm here. Day and night."

"I know."

"I mean it. I'm here for anything."

Silence.

"Monica?"

"Just one more thing I'd like to know, Austin, then I have to hang up."

"Shoot."

"While you were sleeping with me, were you sleeping with Trace?"

He tore out of the house still holding the portable in his hand. The Tahoe turned over instantly. He shot up the mountain road.

"Austin?" Monica listened to the crackling noise on the other end of the line. "Austin? Did you hear me?"

He left the Tahoe's engine running as he bolted across her yard, up the porch and threw open the front door. He ran to the kitchen.

"Austin? Can you hear me?"

"Damn right I heard you."

"What are you doing here?"

"Defending myself. Where the hell did you get some screwball idea about me and Trace?"

"She said you bought the biggest box of condoms in High-statler's."

"So?"

"You didn't use them all with me."

"You are crazy...just like they said."

The wounded look in her face rent his heart.

"Get out!" she shouted.

"You believe that I would fool around? You believe them and not me? What kind of trust is that?"

"I have no reason to trust you."

"And no reason not to. I was planning to finish the box off...in the future. With you. Did you ever think of that?"

Her heart hammered against her ribs. Just the sight of him was more thrilling than she remembered. She could feel the electricity jolting through her like it always did. Damn, she could trust that, couldn't she?

"No, I didn't," she finally replied.

"You know, I think I've been darned noble about all this," he waved his arm in front of him.

"Noble?"

"Yeah. Letting you have your space so you could decide that even if everyone else in your life screwed you over, at least you knew I was on your side."

"That's the conclusion you thought I'd come to?"

He was across the room in two paces. His breath tore out of his lungs like he'd been running the one-eighty. "You bet your ass. It's the only one I'll accept."

He grabbed her wrist ungently and pulled her into his arms. "You feel best right here," he said with fierce low tones that made her forget all reason.

He captured her lips in a rapacious, possessive kiss, slanting his mouth over hers again and again as if devouring her.

And she let him.

He was eager. Very eager as his tongue consumed her, reminding her of every second they'd lost while she'd closeted herself away hoping to understand life. Her life.

He was right. She felt best in the circle of his arms; her

breasts smashed against his hard chest, feeling his heartbeat equal hers. Becoming one with her.

Encircling her arms around his neck, she held his nape, making certain his kiss would never end. She kissed him back, seducing him with her tongue the way he'd taught her. She felt their mutual heat escalate; their bodies' musk scent the air, intoxicating her.

"Monica…"

His sensual gutteral tones set off the time bomb in her loins.

"Tell me you want me." He slipped his hand up her blouse. He cupped her breast, kneading it, cajoling it into the response he expected. He rubbed her nipple between his fingers.

Lightning bolts ripped through her body. "Austin…"

She flung her head back, accepting his hot kisses on her throat, down her chest.

"Say it."

"I want you."

The sound of her blouse buttons popping, then rolling on the floor, distracted her only momentarily. His lips had taken her breast. She could feel her flesh swelling as her veins filled with hot pulsing rushes of blood.

"Take me," she breathed, sinking her hands into his hair, urging his mouth to continue her torment.

Zippers unzipped. Denim fell in puddles at their ankles.

He clamped his hands on her waist and, lifting her, he placed her on the kitchen table.

With his tongue he showed her that torture was his to mete out. Pleasure was hers to receive. He was the giver. She was the taker.

She felt as if she were melting. She leaned back on the table, now that her spine had turned to liquid and her thighs quivered of their own volition.

She was lost to him, as she was swept up in a swirling maelstrom of emotion and physical pleasure. She felt like laughing and crying at the same time. Then came that incredible lightness as if her being were floating out of her body and into another galaxy. She could never be sure if she'd find her way back.

His hands were around her waist again, lifting her off the table, placing her legs around his waist and sliding her down on himself. He was inside her. Filling her. Deliciously stretching her to accommodate him.

He took her mouth again. His tongue pushed inside her, then retreated with the same rhythm as his shaft. Her body became his body. Her needs were his needs. Her desires were his. He served only to please her. She knew it. He knew it.

"This time open your eyes," he groaned, grinding himself into her again.

"No."

"Do it," he demanded.

"Heaven...I have to see..." She was almost there.

She'd never been so much on fire. It was as if his lovemaking to this point had been an initiation. His intensity had never been this strong.

"Look into my eyes. See me..."

She shook her head.

As he pumped himself into her in a series of thrusts, Monica cried out.

"Now look at me!"

She opened her eyes.

She didn't think it was possible to see light so deep down in another person's eyes, but she did. It was sparkling silver like fireworks, but soft and diaphanous like a whisper. She'd been wrong before when she thought she'd seen heaven. Heaven was in his eyes.

"Now you're truly mine...forever." He pushed himself deeper than he thought possible.

She felt him explode. The pulse of it, the heat of it shattered her heart, freeing the love inside.

"Tell me you're mine," he said.

"I'm yours."

He kissed her again.

It was his most demanding kiss of all. This time he wouldn't let her shut him out. This time he was here to stay.

Monica awoke in the morning to Austin's kiss.

"I think we exorcised a few demons last night," he said, lowering his head to the valley between her breasts.

"Which ones?"

"Your distrust of me, for one."

Placing his hands on her ribs, he slid them up, pressing her breasts together where he easily moved from one nipple to the other.

"I had to be sure."

Looking into her eyes, he asked, "I'm not that kind of guy, Monica. Never was. Never will be. Do you think what I do to you is technique?"

"I…don't know."

"Well, it's not. I make love with you. I use my body to show you how special you are to me. I want you to experience things through my touch that you would never know with anyone else."

"I've never been with another man."

"Do you regret that?"

"No."

"Are you sure? I mean, maybe I've been too selfish. You don't have a base of comparison. Maybe I'm cheating you out of that. Maybe you'd like to be with someone else…"

"No!" She put her arms around his neck. "How could there be more than this?"

"You don't know how afraid I was to ask you those questions."

"You? Afraid?"

"Yeah." He slipped his hands under her buttocks and raised her to him.

She opened herself. She was ready.

He filled her instantly.

"I'm all the way inside you," he whispered.

"I know."

"I don't think you really do. I could take you morning, noon and night, and it would never be enough for me. I thought I'd go crazy not having you."

"You said I was crazy."

"I was hurt because I thought you didn't want me."

"I've been confused," she replied as he moved himself inside her without withdrawing. The sensation ignited a deep pulsing, as if a heavy gong reverberated in her soul.

"I promise I'll never say that to you again," he said, pressing himself farther inside.

Her muscles tensed. She closed her eyes to everything except the pulse beat.

She contracted with him.

She released with him.

She arched her back and pulled his mouth down over her breast.

It was coming. Fast. Strong. Like a tidal wave. She was going to drown this time. She held her breath.

He licked and teased her nipples with his teeth, lips and tongue.

His fingers pinched the soft folds of her buttocks.

She heard a roar in her ears.

"Austin!" She pressed her hands into his flanks. "Deeper. Take me deeper." *Higher. Take me with you.*

They exploded together in shuddering rushes of pleasure. He swallowed her breath with his kiss.

She captured his cry.

He vowed to himself he would never leave her.

"I love you, Monica."

She was so stunned she didn't reply. Did she imagine it? Had she wanted to hear it from him so badly, she'd conjured the words in her head? She was too afraid to ask him to repeat it. What if she was right? How would she feel then?

She was a hypocrite, she realized. She'd been demanding the truth from him, from her past, and now she was faced with it. And it scared the hell out of her.

Austin's happiness nearly broke Monica's heart.

He beamed with his love for her. He couldn't do enough for her. He fixed her breakfast in the morning, helped her sift through the fire debris and clear away truckloads of the charred barn remains. Though sweaty and sooty, he would stop working just to look at her or steal a kiss. He whistled as he worked and conjured plans for the barn's rebuilding.

"I wish I'd talked to you about practical matters before this happened."

"Like what?"

"Insurance. You need a good umbrella policy, a couple million would do it. I've got a friend in Chicago..."

"Austin, I can't afford it."

"It's not that expensive. But these days, liability insurance is a must."

She shook her head and let him ramble, not listening to the words as much as she heard the caring tone in his voice. How simple it was to love this man. And yet, how difficult it was to discard the ruler Adelaide and Rose had given her by which to measure men.

She battled her fears like an archangel, fiercely and with strong conviction that what was in her heart was the truth. But it wasn't easy.

What if he leaves me? she fretted. What if I risk my emotions on him and I lose? He's got concrete under his feet. I've got farm soil. We're too different. I cling to the past. He rockets toward the future.

"You know," Austin was still talking when she came out of her reverie, "you're sitting on a gold mine here."

"Gold?"

He straightened his back and wiped the back of his hand across his forehead, streaking it with soot. He squinted his eyes against the afternoon sun and pointed toward the cabin. "The way I figure it, I think there's nearly a half million bucks in that cabin of yours."

A guffaw leapfrogged over her initial chuckle. "That's the most ridiculous thing I've ever heard. Real estate prices here are nowhere near—"

Shaking his head, he interrupted, "Not the house, though it's worth more than you might think. The stuff inside it. The antiques. Correct me if I'm wrong. Those Tiffany lamps? Originals, right?"

"Uh-huh."

"The kitchen chairs. Frank Lloyd Wright. So are the end tables, coffee tables. Early prairie designs. Bird's eye maple."

"How do you know so much?"

"I'm from Chicago," he replied, as if that explained everything.

"I see."

He tossed down a melted piece of metal. "He was a protégé of Louis Sullivan, the architect whose stamp is everywhere in Chicago. 'Course they're tearing down way too much of it to suit me these days. Frank Lloyd Wright cut his teeth in Chicago. Created the prairie look. Stark, clean, functional lines. Like your cabin. Your grandfather knew what he was doing. A real aesthete. I think I would have liked Foster Skye. We have a lot of the same tastes."

Monica braced. "I'm sure of that."

As soon as the words left his mouth, he realized his mistake. "I didn't mean it like that."

Silence.

He closed the distance between them in three strides. "I'm not going to leave you, Monica."

"How do you know? You might change your mind just like he did."

"I know myself better than that. Isn't there anything I can say that will convince you?"

"I don't know," she replied, confusion filling her eyes.

"There's only one way you're ever going to know for certain."

"How's that?"

"Trust me. Wait and see. Invest your time with me. That's the risk you have to take. It's the same one I'm taking with you."

"I don't like risks of any kind."

"Sorry, but it goes with the territory. Besides," he said, pulling her closer, "I fixed it so you'll have to trust me."

"How?"

Pressing his lips to her ear he whispered, "I didn't use a condom last night. You could have gotten pregnant."

"What?" How could she have missed it? Was that why their lovemaking had been more sensitive, more explosive? She didn't know all that much about contraceptives, though she'd gotten the basics from health class in high school. "You did that on purpose?"

"Actually, no. But it wouldn't be so bad would it?"

"Ho! Not for you maybe. But for me. I was just starting to make a few friends in town. I can hear the gossip coming. I'd be just like Mother...." I don't want my child to be a bastard.

He clamped his mouth over hers hoping to dispel her bitterness with his love. His kiss was tender and all consuming.

It washed away her pain.

"No, you're nothing like your mother. I'm not like your father. I'm not leaving. Damn it! I staked my claim when I bought the Harrisons' house. I knew I was searching for something when I moved here, but I didn't know what. Until I laid eyes on you."

"When you were peeping on me, you mean."

Shaking his head, he said, "There was never anything profane in my mind, even at first sight. I thought you were an angel. I know it sounds overly romantic but I was bewitched by you. Although I didn't admit it to myself."

"Why not?"

"I was scared."

"You were—"

"Mmm-hmm. Just like you are now. I didn't want you to leave me. I've been lonely...for a very long time."

"So have I. But I don't want you to want me just because you're lonely."

He caressed her face. "Never. Not a chance. In fact, the opposite is the case. You had to be someone very special to break me out of that. And that's what I want to do for you."

He kissed her deeply then, letting her feel his heart.

"Oh, Austin," she nuzzled her face in the crook of his neck while he kissed the top of her head. "I want to be sure, like you."

"You will be. I'll make certain of it."

"I just don't see how...."

"You will," he said confidently. "You will."

It took two days for Austin to convince Monica they should attend the festival dance that Saturday night. "I don't know how to dance," she said to him over the phone. He'd called her during the long afternoon he spent overseeing the last of the work on his house.

"I'll teach you. It'll be fun."

Fun. What was that? Life had always been so serious for her. Austin was showing her that life was like a diamond with many facets. Turn it one way and it glittered one color, then another quarter turn and a flaw appeared. Just as quickly, however, another rainbow of colors would change everything. He made even the sunrise fascinating.

She was even starting to trust him.

"I'd want to learn before we went to the festival…if that's all right with you."

"Sure, but they'll have a live band. It won't—"

"No!" she retorted adamantly.

"What is it, Monica? You can tell me."

"I just don't want to give any of them reason to—"

"You don't have to say it, love. I understand. I tell you what, when the guys leave tonight, I'll get out my CD's."

"I'd feel more comfortable here. If you don't mind. Then we can have supper and dance some more, if I'm any good."

"You will be," he assured her.

It was dark when he arrived, because the work crews had stayed late, finishing the wood floor in the master bedroom and applying the last coat of paint to the walls.

He parked the Tahoe and smiled at the blaze of lights coming from every room in Monica's cabin. It looked inviting. It looked the way home should be.

He knocked on the screen door, peering into the interior. "Monica?"

"I'm here," she said as the light in the living room was extinguished. "I have a surprise for you."

Cole Porter music played from the antique Victrola as he stood inside a fantasy of sparkling lights. "What the—"

"It was my grandmother's. She only took it out on New Year's Eve when my grandfather was still with her. They used to dance under it, she told me," she said, explaining the 1920s turning mirrored ball suspended from the ceiling. Monica had placed a lamp atop a bookshelf at such an angle so as to illuminate the ball.

She moved out of the shadows, wearing an old sheer white cotton dress whose ankle-length skirt whirled around her legs like rising mist. Her hair and eyes gleamed with a light from within, and for an instant he held his breath. She looked as if she were walking out of a dream. And she was. His dream.

He held out his hand. "I've never seen anyone so beauti-ful."

She went into his arms. "It's the light. Plays tricks on your eyes. Makes you feel like you're moving in space."

"No, this is no trick." His eyes smiled at her.

"What do I do?"

"Keep the toes of your shoes close to mine and let my feet push your feet. Keep your hips close to mine, almost touching me, that way you'll sway when I sway, bend when I bend. My arms will do the rest."

"It sounds as if I don't do a thing."

"Sure you do."

"What's that?"

He grinned mischievously. "Trust me."

His arms were strong as he moved in time with the music. She thought she would have stumbled all over him, but she didn't. He signaled each change of step with his left hand, then when it came to the turns, he tugged on her waist, neatly depositing her where he wanted her.

Dancing with Austin was like making love with Austin. She let him be the guide, and suddenly she felt as if she were floating. It wasn't possible that her feet touched the ground. By the time she heard the strains of "Night and Day," her mind was so deep inside the lyrics, her body was melded so closely to Austin, that she was unaware of herself at all.

"It's like being transported, isn't it?" he whispered.

"Yes. I can almost feel my grandparents' presence as if it were 1929 again and they were so very happy here."

"It was love that built this house, Monica. I've always known that."

"How very sad that love couldn't keep them together."

He held her very close when he said, "Did you ever think that perhaps we're the ones who are supposed to provide that?"

"I don't understand."

"Maybe you and I...we're a fate thing. Like it's our destiny to finish what they started. Maybe it's best we don't know what broke them up. Maybe Foster was just stupid and selfish. Who knows? That's not what's important to us. What is important is that we learn from their mistakes. We have something good and real, Monica. We've got our chance now...let's not throw it away."

She buried her head in his shoulder. "I want to believe you."

Spinning her around, he made her dizzy, forcing her to lose herself in the music. His laughter was melodious, and she laughed with him.

They danced for over an hour before Austin suggested they rest. Monica made coffee, which they shared in the kitchen. Monica studied the contents of her mug for long moments before drinking.

"Didn't you like dancing with me?" he asked.

Nodding, she replied, "Very much so."

"Then why this wary look I see?"

"I guess I'm tired," she lied.

"You'll have to do better than that." He leaned back in the chair. "I've noticed that it's hard for you to let yourself go and enjoy life, isn't it?"

"I wouldn't say that."

"It's okay. I was like that before I came here. So I understand your feelings. But the real truth of the matter is that no matter what I do, what I say, I can't convince you I'm not the boogeyman out to hurt you. You've been circumspect about me from the start." He held up his hand, stopping her protests.

Reaching in his pocket he withdrew an envelope. "I received this letter the other day. After reading it, I realized that part of your distrust in me, if not all of it has been due to circumstances beyond my control. I can't defend myself against your old ghosts. In a way you're guilty of treating me much the same as the citizens of Silver Spur have treated you.''

''That's not true—'' She hesitated.

''Think about it. You judged me and sentenced me according to what you'd heard about Foster Skye. If he was a swindler, then I must be one, as well.''

Sheepishly she looked away. ''I did,'' she admitted.

''Maybe it's more than coincidence this letter arrived from Harriet.''

Monica's eyes widened. ''You've heard from her?''

He offered the letter to her. ''Read it for yourself.''

Monica pulled out the letter and read Harriet's familiar scrawl.

Dear Mr. Sinclair,

I'm writing to thank you for being the answer to our prayers. When your car broke down at our place, Chuck and I thought our life together was over. I hadn't been able to tell any of my friends about our troubles, because folks in Silver Spur are notorious gossips and, frankly, I didn't want to see pity in their faces when they learned I had cancer. Because we had no health insurance, I was convinced there was no hope. When you gave us that cashier's check, Chuck and I fell to our knees. By moving here to Billings, I've been able to receive incredible care. I'm still weak from the radiation, but I was told I would not have to undergo chemotherapy. For that I'm grateful. And to you, too. Your money has paid for all our living expenses and my medical bills. You were overly generous in the price you paid for our house and land, and because of that we've put a deposit on a very nice apartment near a library.

Chuck and I can't thank you enough. We hope you are enjoying your new home in Silver Spur. The people are slow to warm to strangers, but they're good people. I miss my friends very much. Should you meet Monica Skye, your neighbor, please give her my love. I feel guilty for not telling her about my illness, but she was so grief stricken when Adelaide died, I didn't want to burden her with my problems. Frankly, I never thought I'd still be alive.

We're keeping you in our prayers,

Harriet and Chuck Harrison.

Monica looked up from the letter with huge tears in her eyes. "She didn't want to trouble me...." She clamped her hand over her mouth.

"She's a strong lady."

Nodding, Monica replied, "I owe you an apology for doubting your integrity."

"Accepted," he said, reaching for her hand. "Harriet was right about the people here. Maybe you should give them another chance."

"I've been wrong about so many things."

"We're all guilty of that from time to time." He wiped a tear from her cheek. "You know the old saying? The truth will set you free?"

"Uh-huh."

He smiled. "Feels good, doesn't it?"

She returned his smile. "Very."

Fourteen

Monica insisted upon driving her sputtering truck to town the afternoon of the festival. She didn't want to tell Austin she planned to buy a new dress. She wanted to surprise him. But she'd had a devil of a time convincing him it wasn't necessary for him to pick her up so they could drive to town together.

Fortunately his work crew had insisted upon working on Saturday. They wanted to finish the job so they could get paid.

Monica reveled in the idea of having the afternoon to herself. She had telephoned Grace and made an appointment to have Grace help her with her hair and makeup. Grace had suggested she was in dire need of a manicure as well. Believing Grace hadn't steered her wrong so far, Monica agreed.

Arriving in town, Monica was amazed this many cars and trucks existed in Silver Spur and that they were all here for the festival. To her recollection, Monica didn't remember the festival. Perhaps as a child she'd attended, but she doubted it.

"No, surely I would have remembered all this!"

The town square was festooned with red, white and blue pots of flowers; green vine garland interlaced with petunias and daisies encircled the lampposts; huge white wicker baskets of geraniums and bachelor's buttons sat on long tables under white tents. The Victorian gazebo where the band would play was decorated with American flags and Japanese lanterns. Strings of tiny white Christmas lights were being tested and laced through the pine trees around the wooden dance floor where she and Austin would dance tonight.

The sheriff had closed off Central Avenue where the brightly colored canvas of carnival booths lined the sidewalks. A carousel was already in operation, its tinkling nickelodeon music mingling with the harried barks and orders of carnies setting up a Ferris wheel and whirligig.

Fun. It was going to be such fun.

Monica parked her truck three streets over from the town square on Market Street. There was a spring in her step as she walked to the general store. She didn't think about the pain from her burns, nor the loss of her goods. She didn't think about the problems with Trace or Jake or Bill Highstatler's lecherous glares. She thought about Austin and how much she wanted to look pretty for him tonight.

"Are these all the dresses you have?" Monica asked Beatrice Quay, the owner's wife.

"Sure is," she replied without looking up, as she counted out change to another customer.

"There was a pretty blue dress with white embroidered daisies I saw—"

"Sold it," Beatrice cut in roughly.

"And a yellow cotton with a scalloped neckline."

"Sold it. Weeks ago."

Monica's eyes widened. "I'd been admiring them both for the longest—"

"Everything sells for the festival. By nightfall even that ugly navy with the red belt will be gone."

Monica didn't like the way Beatrice always finished everyone's statement for them, but the woman was nearly seventy and she probably wasn't going to change her ways at this point in her life. "Well, thanks just the same."

Monica started to walk out the door. "You don't suppose the church thrift shop would have anything?"

"Sold out before I did."

Dejectedly Monica's eyes fell. "I see."

"Course, there's a new ladies shop over on Elm. Kinda outta the way. She doesn't sell much. Her clothes being so outrageous and all."

"Really? What kind of clothes does she sell?"

"Nothing I'd have in my store, I can tell you."

Monica glanced at the hideous lime green and orange shirtwaist and the bland beige sleeveless, shapeless cotton shift. "I might give it a try What's the name of the shop?"

"Treena's. Can't miss it. It's just a makeshift thing. She's using the old Caplans' house. Lives in the back."

"Enterprising," Monica commented and left. She didn't miss Beatrice's disapproving snort.

Treena's was spelled out in yellow letters against the white clapboard house. In the wide picture window stood two mannequins both wearing slim-fitting summer suits in white, holding black patent-leather handbags, white gloves and black and white umbrellas. There was a new yellow-and-white-striped canopy over the door to keep customers dry. Fake grass had been placed over the sidewalk, and clay pots painted white were filled with fake sculpted cone-shaped trees. Monica pushed the door open, and a little bell tinkled announcing her.

"Hello? Anybody here?"

A pair of white silk curtains parted dramatically. "Well, hello, darling! God! Are you gorgeous or what?"

"Are you Treena?"

"The one and only!" The flame-haired young woman tilted

toward her on very high-heeled shoes, her tight, extremely short skirt seeming to impede her movements. She clanked as she moved, so weighted down with jewelry that Monica was reminded of a prisoner in chains. Her blouse plunged so low Monica wondered if there was much of her expansive breasts she wasn't showing. She extended her hand, a ring on each finger. "Glad to meet you."

Monica tried to smile, but she was too busy staring at Treena's impossibly long eyelashes and nearly black lipstick. "It's nice to meet you. This is my first time in your shop." She looked around at the vacant spaces where she'd expected dress racks to be. All she saw was a lit case filled to overflowing with costume jewelry and a wall of plastic bins containing what she guessed was hosiery, lingerie and scarves.

Treena scanned Monica from head to toe. "Size eight. What are you five foot eight? No, nine," she answered her own question. "A 'summer' with those eyes. Clear reds, electric blues, pastel blues with lots of silver. No." She stuck her finger in the air. "Platinum. That's it! You'll wear platinum."

"You have something?"

"Darling, I have it all." She glided her hands down the sides of her ample breasts, wasp waist and fully rounded hips. She disappeared behind the curtains.

Monica heard rummaging noises. Boxes falling. Coat hangers scraping against metal. "Shoe size? Eight and a half medium. Right?"

"Why, yes." What is this woman? A wizard?

"You got any pearls, honey?"

"No. Not with me."

"Too bad. I can always tell the difference with the real thing. Don't let anybody kid you. There's no substitute for the real thing. And you're it, honey."

"I am?"

Treena emerged with arms laden. Pulling back the curtain and hooking it on a gold rose-shaped holder, Treena motioned to a three-way mirror, a carpeted platform and a straight chair. She placed the shoes, a pair of soft silver low-heeled pumps devoid of decoration on the platform. Next to it, was a palm-sized leather evening bag to match. Silver pantyhose that sparkled in the light. Then over the chair she draped a simple, but elegant dress of the most beautiful silver-blue silk Monica had ever seen.

"Why it looks like my frozen lake in winter."

"You own a lake?"

"Yes," Monica replied mesmerized by the beautiful dress. She'd never owned a dress like this one. She wanted to touch it but didn't dare. "I've only bought my things from the general store. I'm sure this will cost much more than—"

Treena held up her hand. "I take Visa."

"Excuse me?"

Treena dropped her eyes. "Credit cards. I don't suppose you have any."

"No."

"I didn't think so. Seems no one in this one-horse town does."

"How long have you been here?" Monica couldn't help asking.

Treena expelled a sigh. "Six months. At this rate, I'll probably be gone by winter. My clothes don't fit in here. Neither do I," she laughed good-naturedly.

"Didn't you know it was going to be like this when you moved here?"

She shook her head. "No. I inherited the house from my uncle. I was divorced a year ago and was ready for a change of scene. I've got to admit, the scenery here is unbelievable."

"Everybody says that."

"Trouble is…I have to make a living." She shrugged her shoulders and started to pick up the dress.

"No, wait!" Monica smiled. "I haven't tried it on."

Treena returned her smile. "You know, you're right. You're

the first person in here who can do justice to my clothes. God! I wish I had your legs. Another eight inches and I'd tear New York apart!'' She laughed and pulled the curtains shut. ''Take your time.''

When Monica finished dressing, she called to Treena.

''Omigawd, dawling!'' she drawled. ''You're smashing! You got a steady flame? 'Cuz if you don't, you will after this town gets a load of you in that dress. You'd make Cindy Crawford pea green with envy!''

''Cindy who?''

''Never mind.'' Treena went to the jewelry case and returned with a pair of matte silver earrings that looked like oyster shells undulating around a giant white pearl. ''Perfect. That's all I can say. When I'm good. I'm really, really good.''

The dress fell over Monica's curves like fluid. The V-neck bodice was low enough to reveal the crests of Monica's breasts but no more. Its long sleeves fit tightly and ended in a tiny cuff at the wrist. The skirt was ankle length, and when she walked, the fabric moved with her, draping seductively over her thighs, buttocks and hips. There was nothing left to the imagination, yet Monica appeared to be an illusion in the dress. ''You *are* a wizard!''

''And you are a goddess.''

''I have some cash I had planned to spend,'' she looked around the shop, wondering once again if its nakedness was intentional. ''However, I was wondering if you might consider a trade.''

''Trade?''

''Yes. I have some rather rare things you might be interested in…for your shop. To either keep or resell.''

''Yeah? What kind of things?''

''Did you ever hear of Frank Lloyd Wright?''

Grace coordinated a silvery pink pearl nail polish to complement the fabric of the dress. ''You simply have to let me give you a pedicure.''

Monica wanted to draw the line at the manicure. Personal grooming was one thing. Self-indulgence was another.

''You want to ruin those fancy hose the first night out? Then forget the pedicure. I've always said, one pedicure will save a fortune in panty hose.''

''Well, I seldom wear panty hose. There's not much call for them on a ranch,'' she laughed.

''I know, but didn't you say you had a date tonight?''

Monica felt her cheeks warm. ''What's that got to do with—''

''Men like women to paint their toes. It's cuddly sexy.''

''Cuddly sexy?''

''Sure. Turns them on, but doesn't make them go nuts!'' Grace laughed and Monica laughed along with her. ''Tell you what. I'll give you a deal and give you the manicure and pedicure for fifteen dollars altogether.''

''Okay,'' Monica acquiesced. ''And you'll help me with the makeup. I don't think I could ever get the hang of mascara.''

''Sure you will. Just give it time.''

Night had just fallen when Austin drove into town. The sound of honking horns and brakes squealing reminded him of Chicago. ''Some things never change.''

Monica had asked him to meet her outside Grace's Beauty Shop at seven. He was early, but he didn't care. He wanted to see her. This was an important night for them. He was anxious for it to begin.

Monica saw him walking across Main Street from inside the beauty shop. He looked incredibly handsome wearing gray slacks that moved like liquid, breaking just above his highly polished black dress shoes. His shirt was long-sleeved and pale blue and it moved and molded against his muscular chest. ''He's wearing a silk shirt!'' She gasped as Grace joined her at the window.

"By damn! I've never seen a man in silk before."

"Lord, he sure does look handsome."

Grace handed Monica her evening bag and shooed her out the door.

Austin stopped dead in his tracks.

A truck honked twice. "Get outta the way, pard!"

Laughing to himself, Austin sprinted across the street. "You're breathtaking."

"Do you like my surprise?"

"Very much indeed," he said appreciatively. "Turn around, let me see your dress."

"I really shouldn't have spent the money, but—"

He put his finger over her lips. "Forget the money. I'll pay for the dress. Where did you find it?" he asked slipping her arm through his.

As Monica related the comical story about Treena, Austin steered her toward the town square where the band had already started playing.

Monica's experience in Austin's arms that night was unprecedented. Not only did she feel safe and beautiful, she felt wanted and loved. And not just by Austin.

"Hello, Monica. Austin," Doc smiled as he waltzed past them with Myrna.

"Hello, Doc."

"You look lovely tonight, Monica." From Jake Simmons.

"So nice to see you in town more often, Monica. Do we have Austin to thank for that?" From Mrs. Jake Simmons.

"Monica, you're the prettiest darned woman in town," one of Jake's cronies said.

"Did you learn to dance that well in Chicago, Mr. Sinclair?" Beatrice Quay asked Austin as she whirled past in her rotund husband's arms.

One song ran into another, but Monica didn't seem to notice. The entire evening was a night to be remembered for a lifetime. The compliments she received flowed over her like a warm cocoon.

Children raced about holding their sparklers aloft, lovers stole kisses in the clumps of pines and high hedges around the square, and husbands nuzzled wives during romantic ballads. It was the kind of night she'd seen only in picture postcards.

"Aren't you getting tired, sweetheart?"

"Not in the least." She smiled.

"How about thirsty? Hungry?"

"Austin, would you like to stop dancing?"

"Only long enough to get some cake and coffee they're serving under the tent."

"Mmm. Sounds wonderful."

When they walked off the dance floor, their spot was immediately swallowed up by another couple who'd been waiting their turn.

"Gosh! I had no idea there'd be so many people here," she said finding an empty seat on a concrete bench not far from the band shell.

"Tell you what. I'll get the coffee and you keep our seats here."

"Deal."

Bill Highstatler had watched Austin Sinclair like a hawk for over an hour. For a long time he'd thought he wouldn't get his chance, but then he knew there was a God.

"Hi, Monica," Bill said softly.

"Hi, Bill. You look very nice tonight," she said, automatically returning one of the compliments she'd received.

"Glad you think so. How about a dance?"

She shook her head. "I'm waiting for Austin."

"Wait for him on the floor with me."

Before she knew what had happened, Bill's strong arms

were around her waist and she was plastered against his body
from breast to knee.

They weren't moving toward the dance floor.

"What are you doing?" Suddenly, she was frantic.

"Doing what I shoulda done a long time ago. Or maybe
I'm too late. Did pretty boy already have you?"

She opened her mouth to protest. Instantly Bill's hand covered it. Just as quickly they disappeared into the high hedge
and behind the pines.

He shoved her against the ragged pine tree. The bark bit
her back. She struggled. His hand was already up her skirt and
going down inside her panty hose. He clutched her breast and
squeezed hard.

She screamed.

Bill clamped his mouth over hers. "Bitch!"

Austin balanced two Styrofoam cups of coffee and two paper plates with enormous pieces of carrot cake. He'd just lifted
his head searching for Monica and before he saw the empty
concrete bench, he knew.

"She's gone."

He heard her scream at the same moment.

He dropped the coffee into a manicured bed of petunias and
raced toward the sound of her scream. He threw himself
against the hedge, breaking through to the other side.

Monica could smell the liquor on Bill's breath. She slugged
him in the stomach, but he grabbed both her wrists in his huge
hand and twisted them, sending jabs of searing pain down her
arms. With his hips and chest he pressed her harder into the
tree trunk. She felt his fingers probing lower. Writhing like an
angry serpent she managed to foil his intent.

"Come on, Monica. Give it to me like you do for him."

Anger annihilated her pain. She fought like the wild mountain woman he'd claimed her to be since they were kids. She
didn't care if he hated her. She hated him a hundred times
more.

Her scream died in a gurgle in her throat, but she wouldn't give up. Despite his mouth being over hers, she screamed at the top of her lungs.

Austin's hands covered Bill's back like vises. He pulled Bill off Monica in a single angry movement. "You son of a bitch!"

Austin landed a few well-placed blows. Then Bill landed a solid punch to Austin's middle sending him reeling backward. Bill snickered as he walked over, foot back ready to kick the living daylights out of Austin, and suddenly found himself flying into the air.

Austin had grabbed Bill's foot with both hands and upended him. He slammed two more blows to Bill's midsection and backed away.

Putting out his hand for Monica to take, he said, "You ever come near her again, I'll kill you. You hear me, you low-life jerk! No questions asked. You're dead."

"Let's get out of here," Monica said.

"Hell, no! I'm taking this weasel to the sheriff. I'm not going to let him get away with what he did to you."

"Please, Austin. Let's just go. I don't want any trouble. These people have just started liking me, and if they think I stirred up trouble, I'll be right back where I started."

"This isn't your fault."

"Since when did that make anything fair? They've always thought the worst about me."

"Those days are over," he said, going over and taking the unconscious Bill by the collar and dragging him toward the gazebo where he knew he'd find the sheriff.

"What if they're not?"

"Let's just go and see," he said, pulling Bill through the break in the hedge.

Monica couldn't believe Austin was disregarding her wishes. But then, hadn't he been doing that since she'd known him? Always butting into her business. Taking over.

Suddenly she heard voices.

"What the hell's going on, Austin?" Doc's voice said.

"Where's the sheriff?" She heard Austin ask.

"My God!"

"That's Bill Highstatler."

"Yes, it is, Sheriff. He attacked Monica Skye. I want to press charges."

Monica was riveted to the spot. Her hands were shaking, her body ached. She felt violated, rejected and abandoned all at once. She wanted to cry, but she'd be damned if she was going to let them see her weakness.

"Monica?" Austin appeared through the hedges. He held out his hand to her. "Please, come with me, sweetheart. We'll face them together."

"I..." Her eyes darted from side to side like a frightened animal.

He took off his jacket and put it around her shoulders. He kissed the back of her neck. "It's over. No more running. No more hiding. I'm with you now."

She bit her tongue to keep from asking, "But for how long?"

The sheriff's deputies were carting Bill Highstatler away from the crowd and putting him into a squad car. The crowd gasped when they saw Monica's distress.

"Monica and I want to press charges, Sheriff."

"Good for you, Monica," a woman's voice said, and Mrs. Jake Simmons stepped out of the crowd.

"That a girl, Monica!" Treena added and stepped up.

"He's had it coming for a long time, Monica," a man said.

The voices became a chorus, and what she heard stunned her.

"Bill Highstatler's been spreading rumors about Monica for years, Austin. Nobody ever really listened to him, because we all knew they were lies. He's a drunk and a mean-spirited man. Him and that Trace. She's just jealous."

"That's true!" Another voice chimed. "Trace's eaten up with it."

"Guess the Highstatlers never got over old Foster Skye's generosity. They knew they'd never do the things for the valley the way old Foster did. Bill and Vernon's two peas in a pod."

Monica couldn't believe her ears. For so long she'd been guilty of listening to the voice of a few, rather than taking the time to explore the opinions of the many. She was as bad as the gossips. She hadn't spent the time to search out the truth.

She felt ashamed and unworthy of them. "I'm so sorry."

"Why, you ain't got nothin' to be sorry about," Myrna whispered. "We're grateful to you for standing up for yourself."

Monica's slow smile grew brighter. I have done just that, haven't I? Like Austin said. No more hiding.

Austin squeezed her hand. "Hey, everybody! I don't want this thing to ruin our town's festival. Besides, I was planning something very special tonight."

Doc winked at Austin. "And what might that be, Austin?"

He pulled Monica close and gazed at her. "I had planned to do this in private, but that's not possible."

"What are you talking about?"

In a very low voice, he asked, "Would you marry me, Monica?"

"What?" His question took her totally by surprise.

"Now don't get your dander up and be stubborn about this. You know we're meant for each other."

"Well…"

Casting a sidelong glance at the anxious faces around them he continued, "Heck, even they know we should be together. I'd like to tell the good people of Silver Spur that I've adopted them as much as they've adopted me. I love you, Monica. Please say you will."

No one in the crowd breathed as they waited for her answer.

Her eyes smiled first, then she whispered, "I'll marry you."

"Thank God!" Austin shouted. Joy burst from his heart as he gently placed his hand on her cheek and kissed her.

The crowd expelled a rapturous sigh. "Awww." Then they applauded.

Suddenly the sky was lit with brilliant fireworks.

When the kiss ended, the townspeople moved away quickly, giving Austin and Monica their privacy, but as they left they declared to one another, "This is the grandest night this town has ever seen."

"The best."

"We'll take the Tahoe back," Austin said.

"What about my truck?"

Austin stalled for a long moment, looking quite sheepish. "Uh, we need to discuss that."

"Discuss what?"

"The fact that I sold it."

"You did what?"

"If you agree, of course. The guy was into antique cars. It'll be a museum piece. Admit it, Monica. The thing was a death trap. You need a new truck. You said so yourself."

"I can't afford—"

He unlocked the Tahoe with his remote control and cut her off. "I got a great price, and I've ordered you a new truck."

Ramming her hands on her hips angrily, she glared at him. "Is this how it's always going to be with us, Austin?"

He chuckled. "Oh, you mean the part about me always taking care of you and being there for you? That part? Is that what you're talking about?"

"I wasn't thinking about it quite like that."

He moved closer to her as he held the door for her. His eyes fell to her lips. "This is all subject to your approval, of course. I figured you'd want to pick the colors."

Her anger deflated like last night's party balloon. "Well, in that case…"

"Uh-huh. Go on."

"Austin Sinclair…"

"Yes, darling?" His voice was undeniably sensual.

"Am I gonna have one of those little thingamajigs like you have?" she asked, climbing in the Tahoe.

"Yeah, sure. Remote. The works." He shut the door triumphantly after her and hopped into the driver's seat.

He leaned over and kissed her deeply. "I have a problem I want to get solved before we go any further, Monica."

"You mean like whose house are we going to live in?"

"No, that's not a problem because we're going to live in your house where you're happiest."

"You…would do that? After all your hard work on your house?"

"Sure. I'll sell it. Probably make a killing." He pulled her hand to his lips. "That's not the problem."

"You mean like if I'm pregnant already?"

"No, because if you aren't, I intend to make you pregnant before the night's over."

"Austin, you are the most exasperating man! What other problem can there possibly be?"

He looked up to the sky and pointed to the enormous full moon. "Do you suppose by the time that Montana moon fades you might tell me that you love me?"

"But I…"

"No, you haven't."

"But I thought I did."

Shaking his head slowly, he drew her face close to his, brushing his lips against her mouth. "Tell me."

"I love you, Austin. With all my heart."

"Now, say it again."

"I love you."

His breath mingled with hers. "Say it again."

"I love you."

"Again..."

"Austin, how many times do I have to say it?"

"As many as it takes for you to believe I'll never leave you, Monica. Not in this lifetime or the next."

"Oh, that long." She fell into the kiss knowing their love would last forever.

* * * * *

MIRA Books

proudly presents
a new novel from

CATHERINE LANIGAN

In Love's Shadow

For a sneak preview
of this emotional love story
please read on.

And please look for *In Love's Shadow*
in November 1998
wherever books are sold.

"Oh, my God!" Roya cried out as her plate clattered to the highly polished hardwood floor.

He turned around and the impossibly elegant woman gaped at him.

"Look what you've done!" she scolded.

"I…?" He blinked his eyes, clearing the anger from them.

Roya was covered from neck to waist with linguine in basil and olive oil, crab claws and salmon in butter and caper sauce. "My dress is ruined!"

Quickly, he grabbed a linen napkin from the buffet table and anxiously, clumsily began wiping down her dress. "I'm sorry. I didn't see you standing there."

A clump of smoked salmon hit the floor. He tried to catch the pellet-sized capers with his left hand and grasped Roya's breast.

The olive oil and melted butter had seeped through the gold organza bodice, and the fabric had matted to her bare skin. She could feel the heat of his hand against her flesh as if she were naked.

Indignation transmuted to desire in a millisecond.

Roya held her breath. Too much wine had made her light-headed. She flushed.

He dropped his hand abruptly, the words he was about to say caught by the smoky intensity in her blue eyes. There was only one thing he could think to do. He kissed her.

He'd meant for it to be a segue to his offer to pay for her dry cleaning bill. It was supposed to be a trifling peck, a holiday greeting, no more binding than sending a Christmas card to a client.

After all, he was a man of numbers, an accounting genius, a businessman's man. Romance was an illusion, just like in the movies and fiction. But *he* was firmly based in reality; kisses meant nothing to him.

Until now.

It wasn't her full lips, nor their slight tremble that turned him inside out. Nor was it the spice and vanilla scent she wore, somewhere between her full breasts, that invaded his mind. It wasn't her beauty, classic and flawless as it was.

It was the salty tear trickling down her cheek that sucked him from his world into hers. He drank it. Consumed it. Harbored it. Knowing she was part of him now.

He pulled her into him, pressing her body against his and forcing her to meld with him. He splayed his hands across her back, needing to memorize every inch of her, then slanted his mouth over hers, invading her with his tongue. Claiming her. He needed to know her taste, her texture, her responses, as he forced himself deeper. Then deeper still.

His mind was altered. Totally and completely. He fought for some clarity but could find none.

His hand tightened around her breast. He felt her push her flesh against him, filling his palm, overflowing his fingers.

She was a stranger. And yet nothing had ever seemed more natural to him than filling himself with this woman.

Vaguely Roya remembered that she was at a party. But what kind and where, she didn't know. She'd lost her mind, been transformed into a mass of physical, chemical, sexual response.

But in a strange way it all made sense. She'd been starved for affection, attention, sex, for so long that her body had gone into a kind of sexual shock. She craved this sweet man's kiss. Not even when she first met Bud had he kissed her with such possessiveness, such insatiable need.

This stranger kissed her as if she were the last woman on earth and he was going to die in the morning. As if the taste of her lips, the heated press of her breast against his hand, would be the last things he remembered before death.

There was no other explanation.

Then reality hit her like ice water. She had to leave—right now. If she didn't, she'd be to blame for what happened after that. And something would happen. She knew it in every bone of her body. She was more than vulnerable right now. She was hurt and neglected; she was angry at Bud. It was no wonder she'd reacted to this man like she had—she was starved for affection.

He was the most lethal man she'd ever met. And for the rest of her life she knew she'd never forget this moment. Never forget this man!

Take 2 bestselling love stories FREE

Plus get a FREE surprise gift!

Special Limited-Time Offer

Mail to Silhouette Reader Service™

P.O. Box 609
Fort Erie, Ontario
L2A 5X3

YES! Please send me 2 free Silhouette Desire® novels and my free surprise gift. Then send me 6 brand-new novels every month, which I will receive months before they appear in bookstores. Bill me at the low price of $3.49 each plus 25¢ delivery and GST*. That's the complete price, and a saving of over 10% off the cover prices—quite a bargain! I understand that accepting the books and gift places me under no obligation ever to buy any books. I can always return a shipment and cancel at any time. Even if I never buy another book from Silhouette, the 2 free books and the surprise gift are mine to keep forever.

326 SEN CH7V

Name	(PLEASE PRINT)	
Address		Apt. No.
City	Province	Postal Code

This offer is limited to one order per household and not valid to present Silhouette Desire® subscribers. *Terms and prices are subject to change without notice. Canadian residents will be charged applicable provincial taxes and GST.

CDES-98

In **July 1998** comes

THE
MACKENZIE
FAMILY

by *New York Times* bestselling author

LINDA
HOWARD

The dynasty continues with:

Mackenzie's Pleasure: Rescuing a pampered ambassador's daughter from her terrorist kidnappers was a piece of cake for navy SEAL Zane Mackenzie. It was only afterward, when they were alone together, that the real danger began....

Mackenzie's Magic: Talented trainer Maris Mackenzie was wanted for horse theft, but with no memory, she had little chance of proving her innocence or eluding the real villains. Her only hope for salvation? The stranger in her bed.

Available this July for the first time ever in a two-in-one trade-size edition. Fall in love with the Mackenzies for the first time—or all over again!

Available at your favorite retail outlet.

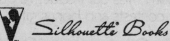

Silhouette Books

The World's Most Eligible Bachelors are about to be named! And Silhouette Books brings them to you in an all-new, original series....

World's Most
Eligible Bachelors

Twelve of the sexiest, most sought-after men share every intimate detail of their lives in twelve never-before-published novels by the genre's top authors.

Don't miss these unforgettable stories by:

Dixie Browning

MARIE FERRARELLA

Jackie Merritt

Tracy Sinclair

BJ James

RACHEL LEE   Suzanne Carey

Gina Wilkins

VICTORIA PADE

MAGGIE SHAYNE   *Anne McAllister*

Susan Mallery

Look for one new book each month in the
World's Most Eligible Bachelors series beginning
September 1998 from Silhouette Books.

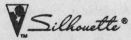

Silhouette®

Available at your favorite retail outlet.